Doctor Dread

by
Ibne Safi

Translated from the Urdu by
Shamshur Rahman Faruqi

Published by

in association with

TRANQUEBAR

Blaft Publications Pvt. Ltd.
4/192 Ellaiamman Koil St.
Neelankarai
Chennai 600041 India
blaft.com

Tranquebar Press
Venkat Towers, 165, P.H. Road, Maduravoyal, Chennai 600095
No.38/10 (New No.5), Raghava Nagar, New Timber Yard Layout,
Bangalore 560026
Survey No. 1/E, Jaipur House, Mona Ali Industrial Area, Moula Ali,
Hyderabad 500040
23/181, Anand Nagar, Nehru Road, Santacruz East, Mumbai 400055
47, Brij Mohan Road, Daryaganj, New Delhi 110002
westlandbooks.in

First published 1957 by Asrar Publications as
Doctor Dread © 1957 Estate of Ibne Safi

First published in English by Blaft Publications in association with
Tranquebar Press 2011

English translation and all editorial content © 2011 Blaft Publications
All rights reserved.

ISBN 978-93-80658-41-4

Cover design: Anjana, Kaveri Lalchand, Vishal Rawlley
Inside page layout: Kaveri Lalchand, Rakesh Khanna

Printed at Aegean Offset Printers, Greater Noida

Acknowledgements

Blaft Publications would like to thank the following people for their invaluable help in bringing out these English editions: Ahmad Safi and the rest of Ibne Safi's family; Mohammed Hanif, who runs the fan website www.ibnesafi.info; Kaveri Lalchand, Nisha Ravindranathan, and Gayathri G. for their editorial input; and all the Safi experts and fans who advised us, including Khurram Ali Shafique, Musharraf Ali Farooqi, Mahmood Farooqui, Irfan Ahmad, and Alexander Keefe.

The cover of this book incorporates the original painting from the cover of the 1957 Allahabad edition of *Doctor Dread* by Siddiqui Artist. It also includes the trademark logo of Asrar Publications, Ibne Safi's publishing house (with offices in Karachi and Lahore), designed by Mustafa Mirza.

Translator's Note

Ibne Safi was born Asrar Ahmad on July 26, 1928, in Nara, an ancient village in Allahabad. As a young, aspiring writer, he wrote poetry, short stories and humorous pieces—signing most of them "Asrar Naravi", but also using many pseudonyms. He came into his own when he was commissioned to write a short detective novel every month for a series called *Jasusi Dunya* ("The World of Detection", or "The World of Espionage") issued from Allahabad. The first novel appeared in March, 1952.

This novel, *Dilaer Mujrim* ("The Brave Criminal"), which introduced Inspector Faridi and his sidekick Sergeant Hameed, became an instant success, the names of Faridi and Hameed soon passing into everyday conversation in the Urdu world. Ibne Safi soon migrated to Pakistan with his mother (his father had already been there since 1947), but he continued to produce novels for *Jasusi Dunya*, and also for his own publishing enterprise, Asrar Publications, publishing his novels simultaneously in India and Pakistan.

In 1955, he commenced another series of novels, called the Imran Series, featuring Ali Imran, an ostensibly frivolous young man who is in fact X-2, the head of a super-secret intelligence agency. Soon, Imran too passed into the common vocabulary of Urdu speakers.

Apart from these heroes, aficionados cherished many of the

other bizarre, unusual, and comic characters which enliven Ibne Safi's narratives.

Ibne Safi's enormous success has been attributed to many things: his humour, the topicality of his stories and relevance to world politics as reflected through the consciousness of a third-world narrator, his memorable characters, his fast-paced narrative, and his original and imaginative situations. Perhaps the most arresting characteristic of the universe he created is its plenitude. The Urdu short story writer Khalid Jawed says that in his two series, Ibne Safi created two *mahakavyas* for modern times.

Although some of his earliest stories were modelled on English detective and adventure novels, even borrowing from them in places, the vast bulk of Ibne Safi's oeuvre must be regarded as original, and entirely native to the subcontinent.

Ibne Safi's most famous character is Inspector Ahmad Kamal Faridi, an aristocrat whose passionate interest in criminology leads him to obtain a degree in that discipline from the University of Oxford, followed by extensive work in forensic laboratories. He knows many languages, is an expert at martial arts, and has deep knowledge of many arcane subjects. He lives in a palatial home where he keeps snakes and many dozens of pedigree dogs. His house also has a well-equipped laboratory and an extensive library. He frequently uses disguise as a means of gathering facts or to reach the criminal he is pursuing. He is somewhat of a loner, usually working without much outside support.

Faridi's manner is generally forbidding, even cold, but he is not devoid of humour. A confirmed bachelor, he likes luxury cars and appreciates the finer things in life—except that women rarely move him, if they ever do at all. In contrast to Faridi, his sidekick Sajid Hameed is a happy-go-lucky kind of young man. A natty dresser, he likes the company of young women, but never goes beyond harmless banter, mild flirtation and ball-room dancing. He avoids work whenever he can, and will even shirk it if he thinks he can get away with it. He lives in Faridi's house and behaves as if he owns it. He sometimes seems to regard Faridi as a father figure.

The most memorable feature of Hameed's character (and perhaps of the whole *Jasusi Dunya* series) is his wacky, zany, but also occasionally wounding humour. He spares no one, not even Faridi. His abundant sense of humour never leaves him, and in fact can become even more outrageous when the circumstances are dire.

At the beginning of the series, Faridi seeks and accepts an appointment as an inspector out of his love for criminal detection. Sergeant Hameed is assigned to him as his assistant. They become more and more renowned over the years, but remain Inspector and Sergeant, until accepting honorary ranks as Colonel (for Faridi) and Captain (for Hameed) after the capture of Gerald Shastri, a notorious super criminal, in *Jangal ki Aag* ("Forest Fire"), the thirty-seventh novel in the Faridi series.

Ibne Safi died in Karachi on 26 July, 1980, his fifty-second birthday, having completed 125 Faridi novels and 116 Imran novels, as well as several books of humour, satire, and poetry.

—Shamsur Rahman Faruqi

A Mysterious Conversation

There was the sound of a vehicle coming to a halt, the crunch of gravel under heavy wheels, and the sound of a horse's hooves stamping heavily on the ground. Shaheena opened the window and looked out, but could see nothing on account of the darkness that enveloped the grounds of the bungalow. She had given instructions for the porch light to be kept burning all night, but the servants seemed to have ignored her orders. She moved away from the window, determined to fight it out with her mother tonight.

For the past several nights, Begum Irshad had been coming home very late, using the horse and carriage instead of the car for her nocturnal excursions. It was unusual enough that she was staying out so late, let alone using the carriage, which no one had ever seen her ride before. It was Shaheena who had a penchant for using the carriage; she often rode it in the evenings for pleasure.

Shaheena left her room and walked through the corridor to the outer verandah. Someone was stepping onto the verandah from the porch. She could see nothing more than a vague shadow against the background of dim starlight.

"Who's there?" Shaheena's voice was trembling.

The shadow stopped moving.

"Who's there? Answer, or... or I'll shoot!" she bluffed.

"Shaheena?" came a low, hoarse voice.

"Mummy? Mummy, is that you?"

The shadow passed her and disappeared into the dark corridor. Shaheena followed the shadow into a room, where the lights were switched on—by her mother.

Begum Irshad was wrapped from head to foot in a dark cloak. Even most of her face was hidden. She did not look her daughter in the eye. Her lips were cracked and dry, and her skin looked pale.

"Mummy! I'm shocked..." Shaheena said quietly.

"Oh, it's nothing, you know. I... I just had to go out on an important errand."

"But you never used to take the horse and carriage."

"Just a whim, I suppose."

"And I can't help but notice, you've been coming home very late these days."

"Go to bed. Go; this isn't any of your business," Begum Irshad said, irritated.

"If *I* didn't come home until nine o'clock at night, you would make it your business."

"Go to bed, child. Leave me alone, for God's sake."

"I've also noticed that you've been looking nervous and worried for several days now."

"Shaheena, please go to your room, dear. I don't feel well enough for this discussion at the moment."

"What is it that you're hiding from me, Mummy? I don't think you've ever kept secrets from me before."

"Secrets? I have no secrets from you, dear girl. Actually, the truth is... I think it's just nervous tension." As soon as she said this, the harassed look disappeared from Begum Irshad's face; she appeared calmer now that she had found a plausible excuse for her strange behaviour. She drew a deep breath and went on, "Sometimes staying at home feels oppressive. So I take the carriage out and go for a long drive." She paused for a second or two, then cracked a smile. "You'd be surprised. I drive the buggy myself!"

"But why don't you consult a doctor?"

"It's just some temporary mood swings, I think. I'm quite all right otherwise. Nothing has really happened to justify consulting a doctor."

Begum Irshad's explanation obviously didn't satisfy Shaheena. On the contrary, she was even more worried now than before.

"Go... go back to bed," Begum Irshad repeated gently. Shaheena kissed her mother on the forehead and left the room. She walked down the long corridor towards her own bedroom, switching the lights off one by one.

Suddenly, she heard the sound of stealthy footsteps. She stopped and stood still. It sounded as though some-one was walking out through the hallway to the main door, which opened to the outer verandah. She stood in the dark, quiet and motionless.

The sound of footsteps ceased. Shaheena now moved carefully toward the main door, but she did not switch on any lights. She saw the dark shadow again on the porch; it could be none other than Begum Irshad. She was still wrapped in her dark cloak.

Shaheena stood, hugging the wall and making no sound. She observed the shadow as it stepped off the porch onto the open lawn. Then it turned toward the part of the grounds where the animals were kept. Shaheena crept out and followed her mother, keeping close to the wall; her dress often caught on the thorny bushes, slow-ing her progress, but she was careful to avoid being seen by Begum Irshad.

Hidden behind the jasmine hedge, which was as tall as a man, she could see her mother clearly; but her mother would not have been able to see her, even if she had deliberately turned around to look.

The hedgerow ended near the animals' enclosures, where her mother had stopped.

"You have been far too slow," Shaheena heard a man's voice say, in English. There was silence for a few seconds, and Shaheena could hear the loud beats of her own heart.

Then she heard her mother speak: "I can't do it."

"You have no choice," the man answered.

There was no answer from Begum Irshad.

"Speak. Why are you silent? Could nothing be done even today?"

"No," her mother said.

"Then your darkest days are now upon you."

"Please... please don't ruin me."

"It won't be me who's responsible. You'll be the one who is the cause of your own ruin."

"Oh God, oh God! What will I do?"

"You must do what you've been asked to do," the man said coldly, "for you must be aware of my power! I've made a woman of your status go wandering around on foot through the city's stinking alleys."

"Please, have some mercy," Begum Irshad implored.

"I am capable of mercy, but on the condition that my orders are strictly carried out. And by the way—you'll never find him. He is alive, though; don't delude yourself with the notion that he is dead."

Silence ensued. Shaheena could feel her heart thumping and the blood pulsing through her head. She opened her eyes wide, trying to catch sight of her mother's tormentor, but she saw no one. Then she saw her mother going back to the house. In a little while Shaheena heard the front door close.

She stood, rooted to the spot, wondering who the man could have been. His English speech and accent betrayed his foreign origin, but nothing else. Why was he terrorizing her mother? Why was he making her wander through stinking alleys on foot? Begum Irshad was a rich widow, highly regarded in the upper echelons of society. She was also a Member of Parliament. Everyone in the city knew the name of Begum Irshad, MP, for she was always at the forefront of any philanthropic or social welfare projects.

Shaheena remained standing there in the open, lost in thought. It had not occurred to her yet that with the front door closed, she would have a problem getting into the house and reaching her bedroom. She didn't have the courage to go out and investigate the place where her mother had spoken to the mysterious stranger.

After some time, she retraced her steps and realized that she would have trouble getting back into the house without letting her mother know that she had followed her into the grounds. Fortunately, she'd left her bedroom window open, but it was five feet above ground level. She didn't want to spend the rest of the night on the verandah, so she had to climb in.

Shaheena slept fitfully. The memory of the evening's events woke her up repeatedly, enveloping her brain in an unknown fear. She knew that her mother would not take her into her confidence, and this made her even more anxious.

The next morning, she rang up Anwar, the crime reporter.* She knew him well; she also knew that he often undertook freelance investigations, though like any professional expert, he charged substantial fees even for a

---

* Anwar is introduced in *Jasusi Dunya* #12, *Maut ki Aandh* ("Death Storm"), along with Rasheeda—his next-door neighbour and colleague, to whom he is perpetually in debt. The pair were the protagonists of five consecutive novels, while the usual detective heroes, Hameed and Faridi, were on vacation in Europe. – Ed.

casual consultation. She requested Anwar to come home to Irshad Manzil, saying she wanted just fifteen minutes of his time to discuss an important case. But Anwar flatly refused. If she wanted to meet, he told her, she would have to come to *his* place at four o'clock that afternoon.

Shaheena felt slighted. She was a modern girl with an active social life, and very popular. No one had ever refused a request from her before. But she held her tongue, because she needed Anwar's services.

She rang the bell of Anwar's flat at the appointed time, and was received by him civilly enough. Having heard her tale, he made a face and said, "So what's there to worry about? It's not uncommon for the romantic peccadilloes of youth to drive people to write poetry in their old age."

"I don't understand."

"What's there not to understand? What sort of problem could possibly arise for a rich lady like Begum Irshad? What kind of a man could force her to sneak around, wandering on foot though the city's stinking alleys? That man could very well be a blackmailer, couldn't he?"

"That's what you have to find out."

"And what happens once I do?"

"Legal and criminal proceedings will be initiated."

"Why do you suppose Begum Irshad hasn't initiated them herself?"

"I don't know."

"Is there no grey matter underneath that beautiful head of curly hair?" Anwar smiled derisively. "Would it hurt so much for you women to spend just a fraction of the time you spend making yourselves look beautiful trying to improve your brains instead?"

Shaheena bristled. "I didn't come here for a schoolmaster's lecture."

"Okay then, scoot. No one's stopping you."

"You've started putting on a lot of airs."

"No, I've always had them—even back when I was so poor that I spent most of my nights on the pavement. The best way to keep me happy is to loosen up your purse strings. In other words, let there be a retainer on the table first."

Shaheena glared at him with hateful eyes. Then she took out a bundle of notes from her purse and threw it on the table.

"Ten thousand," she said.

Anwar rang the bell. A servant boy entered. "Tea for me," Anwar ordered. "Madam, would you care for tea or coffee?"

"No, nothing. Don't try my patience. Let's get down to business."

Anwar waved the boy off, then said, "Madam, what I was trying to explain was this: if Begum Irshad were in a position to appeal to the law, there would be no need for her to go stumbling about in the city's dirty underbelly."

"So what can be done?"

"It is possible for the blackmailer to be removed from her path, but it'll be a tough task... and it's bound to cost a pretty packet."

"Money, money, again the money!" Shaheena stared hard at him.

"No, I have no doubts about the money. After all, it's Miss Shaheena Irshad I'm speaking to. So you're convinced that last night's visitor was a foreigner?"

"He sounded like one."

"English?"

"I am not too good with accents. I can only distinguish a native from a non-native."

"All right. Do you know of any foreigners among your mother's acquaintances?"

"Well, there are many." She fell into thought. "But yes, there are two in particular..."

"Which two?"

"I can think of two who are not above suspicion. My mother doesn't like them, but they still keep dropping in on her."

"I don't think I'll bother asking again who they are," Anwar said, with some irritation.

"A father and son—English. Their names are Roger and Hunter Dunkitale. They've recently arrived from England, and have been interested in securing my mother's collaboration in some industrial venture."

"And why does Begum Irshad disapprove of them?"

"Well, they're quite stupid. They should really be named Donkeytails, they're so brainless."

"You would know their voices?"

"I can't say for certain."

"Was it one of them you heard, yesterday night?"

"I can't really judge. I was very upset, not in my right mind."

"What will Begum Irshad do if she discovers that I'm investigating her?"

"It doesn't matter to me. As long as my name doesn't come up."

"Why?"

"Because she wants me kept in the dark about all this."

"Okay. I'll look into it."

"It's my birthday the day after tomorrow," Shaheena said. "I'll send you an invite. Maybe you'll have a good opportunity then, among the crowd, to try and learn more."

Anwar reflected for a few moments. "Yes, I think that makes sense."

"Now tell me about your fees. How much will you charge?"

"I can judge that only after I've run through this ten

thousand." Anwar gestured toward the bundle of notes on the table.

"Why should you be so enamoured of money? I never could understand your fascination for it."

"Ah, money!" Anwar drew a deep, cold sigh. "Because it's so uncertain when any of it will come to me. Only this morning I was wondering if I was going to have to seduce the landlord's wife—the rent for this flat is already four months overdue."

"You lie."

"I won't argue with you this evening. After all, there's more money to be expected from you."

"So you'll start work today?"

"I'll start right now. And I'll begin my work by inter- rogating you. First question: Do you know of any friend or acquaintance of Begum Irshad who comes from a dif- ferent class of society?"

"What's that supposed to mean?"

"It means, does she have any friends that she might be looking for in the slums? Why else would she be wan- dering on foot through the city's filthy alleys?"

"I get it," Shaheena said heatedly. "You want to hold us up for ridicule!"

"I seek information. That's all."

"Well, I know of nobody like that."

"But doesn't my question land close to what you already suspect?"

"Maybe that's what you imagine..."

"No, I'm not imagining anything. You suspect the same thing I suspect. If that wasn't the case, you would have approached the police."

Shaheena made no reply. After a few moments of silence, Anwar spoke again: "The little follies committed in youth often become a noose around one's neck in old age."

"You're being impertinent."

"Quite true. I won't contradict you... after all, you're likely to be a source of further income."

"No, I don't think I will be. I'll go explore some other avenues. If I hire you, you'll just go on insulting us."

"By all means, go. There's your money, and you know the way out. In fact, that's precisely the reason I haven't touched that money yet. Had the case been a normal one, I wouldn't have been impertinent with you."

"You're cracked. No doubt about it."

"Since the deal seems to have fallen through, I don't have to accept comments like that anymore."

"I say you had better take this case or I'll just shoot you dead!"

"Before we part, a word of advice: Never threaten a man again. But of course, there are no real men in your class of people."

"Anwar!"

"I'm listening."

"For God's sake, help me. Mummy is in danger. I beg you!"

Anwar picked up the bundle of money and stuffed it in his pocket. He stared hard at her for a long moment, then said: "Go now. I'm on the job. Soon you'll be informed of the results. But look, don't forget that invitation to your birthday party."

Shaheena made no reply. She was lost in thought.

Madness

Captain Hameed increased his pace... but the girl was like a will-o'-the-wisp. Around the very next turn, she disappeared, as though she had never existed at all.

Hameed breathed a deep sigh, raised his head, and looked to the heavens, as if the world had treated him with unimaginable cruelty. He stopped at the crossroads for a minute or two, and then walked away in the direction opposite the one he had been facing.

He hadn't been following the girl of his own choice, or on account of his flirtatious nature. In fact, he was on an assignment. For the past one week, he had been gathering information about her—though not openly, and certainly not by asking her questions. He hadn't even spoken to her, for Colonel Faridi's instructions had been very clear and strict. Were it not for those orders, Hameed felt sure that by now he would have managed to take the girl dancing several times in all the best ballrooms of the city.

As beautiful as she was, Hameed hadn't yet been able to determine her nationality or ethnicity. She was of fair complexion, with green eyes. She always wore a skirt, suggesting that she was a Westerner. Hameed found the way she walked very attractive. Among the other things he liked about her was the fact that she didn't wear makeup, as most girls did. Nor did she have long nails. Occasionally she seemed to use just a hint of red on her lips, but that was all.

Hameed walked on, lost in thought about the girl. Faridi hadn't been forthcoming about the whys and wherefores of the "surveillance", if it could be called that. Hameed knew only this: that she lived in the Shamshad Building, that she worked in a local firm, and that her name was Mary Singleton. Hameed was under the impression that she did not have a very wide circle of friends.

That was all that Hameed had been able to unearth about her—but the girl struck him as mysterious. And today she had really outdone herself. It was as if the earth had opened to swallow her up, or she had somehow dissolved into thin air. Hameed was certain that she hadn't gone into any of the buildings in the neighborhood. He wondered if she had known that she was being watched.

These days, Faridi seemed to be obsessed with surveillance and shadowing. He was having as many as eighteen or twenty people in the city watched with varying degrees of intensity. Hameed was thankful to his boss that he had at least allotted him a girl as his mark, for there was no assignment more tedious and boring than having to tail someone.

He stopped in front of a phone booth; then, after a moment's deliberation, he went in. He dialled Inspector Rekha's home number and found her at home, as he had expected.* Doing a perfect imitation of Faridi's voice, he ordered Rekha to come to the Arlecchino within fifteen

---

* Inspector Rekha Larson is an ambitious junior officer first introduced in *Jasusi Dunya* #53, *Surkh Da'irah* ("The Red Circle"). She has feelings for her boss, Colonel Faridi, which she sometimes has difficulty hiding, though Faridi never evinces any interest. – Ed.

minutes. Rekha didn't even pause to inquire why she was being summoned there.

Coming out of the phone booth, Hameed hailed a cab, and reached the Arlecchino a few minutes later. Truth be told, he was, by this time in life, quite fed up with the standard sorts of entertainment on offer at the local restaurants and hotels. But he had no choice. Where else could he go?

And could he really hope to enjoy himself by seeking out the company of Inspector Rekha Larson of the Criminal Investigation Department? These days, Rekha was utterly fed up with him. It was for this reason that he had pretended to be Faridi when he called her on the phone.

Hameed sat down at a corner table where Rekha's eye wouldn't fall on him directly as she entered. A little while later, he saw Rekha at the door. Entering the hall, she cast her eye around the room and noticed Hameed in the corner. Hameed turned his face away from her, as if he wasn't happy to see her there. Rekha walked on into the recreation hall; Hameed remained where he was. A few minutes later she came back into the dining hall and stood for a few moments, uncertain as to what she should do next.

Finally she approached Hameed and asked: "Where is the Colonel?"

"I have no idea." To Rekha's surprise, Hameed sounded serious and polite. "I've been here for half an hour waiting for him. He told me on the phone to join him here at the Arlecchino."

"That's what he told me too," Rekha said, looking around. She seemed to be trying to decide whether she should choose a table to sit by herself or share Hameed's table.

"Come, sit," Hameed said.

Reluctantly, Rekha took a chair opposite Hameed, who didn't respond with the expected joke or sarcastic remark. Rekha was a little unnerved by this new Hameed.

"When did he phone you?" he asked.

"About half an hour ago," Rekha said.

"How aggravating. And how foolish of me to not have resigned by now," Hameed said with feigned disgust. "I've had enough of this job."

"Maybe he required our presence here, for some reason we don't know about yet."

"These maybes and maybe nots are making my life unbearable."

"Then why don't you quit?"

"Do you really think I could hope to quit and have any sort of leisurely life after that? Father Hardstone would never allow it."*

"So what are the current affairs?"

"Oh, all my affairs end up the same way. Every single girl I meet starts talking about marrying me!"

Rekha made a sour face. "That's my cue to exit."

"But you're the one who asked me about my current affairs!" Hameed protested.

"I meant what case are you working on."

"Oh, it's a suitcase." Hameed made an equally sour face. "Full of scorpions. Rekha, don't you ever get bored?"

"Yes, when you start spouting garbage, I do."

Hameed's only reply was to heave a wistful sigh.

After a few moments, Rekha said, "You seem a little dispirited nowadays. Why is that?"

"What's it to you? I could be in hell, and you wouldn't care."

"No, I wouldn't. Not at all. Please go there."

---

* Hameed often refers to Faridi as "Father Hardstone" when he is feeling overworked and put-upon. – Ed.

"Even there in hell, I will sigh mournful sighs of long-ing for you."

"Sure you will," Rekha smiled. "But really? You know how to sigh mournful sighs of longing?"

"I do. I sigh very good sighs of longing. In fact, if you've got a bicycle tyre that needs inflating, just bring it to me."

"How long will you be here?"

"Until Father Hardstone arrives."

"This is the first time this has happened to me. The Colonel's never done this before, asking me to report somewhere and then not showing up himself."

"Maybe he found himself somebody else, after he phoned you."

"You're really past the limit," Rekha said angrily.

"Hush, lower your voice a little. The people at the next table might mistake you for my shrewish wife, and then my future prospects will become dark indeed. Up till now, I've been cultivating my reputation among all the girls of the city as an available bachelor."

"I'm not staying here any longer."

"I'm stubborn enough to follow you wherever you go, so you might as well just remain sitting where you are."

"You're a perfect ass."

"Certainly," Hameed nodded vigorously. "I've never denied it. And yet, I'm still not married."

"Do you have anything else to offer besides this idle talk?"

"Why not? I have a bank balance too. But no one seems to take any notice."

"Ever seen your face in a mirror?"

"Every morning and every evening. I keep hoping to find your name written there on my forehead, to prove that we are destined to be together... but I haven't seen it yet."

"You're in luck. My name's inscribed on the soles of

my shoes—and you're destined to get whacked on the head with them."

"God be praised! So you've become a printing press, now?"

"And you've become completely intellectually bankrupt."

"That's correct. That's precisely why I want you to dance a couple of numbers with me; otherwise I fear I may suffer a mental breakdown today."

"I'm not interested in that foolishness. In fact idiots who like to dance make me want to laugh."

"You go try to impress Colonel Hardstone by telling him that. But unfortunately, he still won't give a damn about you... Oh, ho! Wait a second, shh!" Hameed shut his mouth tight. He was looking over Rekha's shoulder at something, or someone. Rekha turned, too, following Hameed's stare, but couldn't figure out what had startled him.

"What's the matter?" she asked in a low voice.

"What's that girl doing with Anwar?" he murmured to himself.

"Who are you talking about? Oh, that one! But who is she?"

"She's a young and pretty girl. As opposed to an old and ugly one."

"You were about to say something to annoy me. Then suddenly you changed the subject."

"Oh dear. Something meant to annoy you... hmm. Should I go back to the issue of Colonel Hardstone standing you up?"

"You're an uncouth oaf."

"Why, what flaws do you see in me?"

"Shut up."

"My dear, the Colonel may be regarded as the most unfathomable man of the century. On the other hand, *I* may well be regarded as the most unfathomable man of all the centuries to come. But let's drop this matter for the time being. My question is: Why is Shaheena here with Anwar tonight?"

"What, you wish she was with you instead?"

"Pah. In your presence, I wouldn't even make eyes at an elderly goat."

"And what if I get tough, and start cursing you with some choice language?"

"Then I'll get tough as well, and start slapping you with some choice slaps. Come on, go ahead, start."

Rekha turned her attention back to Shaheena and Anwar. The latter looked resplendently magnificent in a black suit and a starched white shirt. Shaheena, on the other hand, was dressed in a sari with a blouse so skimpy that Hameed wondered how she hadn't contracted pneumonia yet. A crazy thought crept into his head.

"Do these women chew on burning coals?" he asked Rekha.

"Why, what are you talking about?"

"It's terribly cold out, and yet this woman Shaheena is wearing a blouse barely the size of my hand. Half her belly is showing."

Rekha looked at him pityingly. "Well of course you don't think she came like that? She must have checked her coat at the entrance."

"But isn't it cold in here, too?"

Rekha said nothing.

A few moments later, Hameed said, "If you don't agree to dance with me tonight, I will exact a most terrible revenge."

Rekha shook her head violently, as if there was a mosquito humming away annoyingly in her ear. But Hameed wouldn't give up. "You don't understand," he said. "If Anwar manages to partner that pretty young thing for a dance and I'm left sitting here, he'll have a chance to act superior and look down upon me."

"That's of no concern to me."

"Okay then, I'll sort you out."

Rekha really lost her temper now. "What's this high-handedness? Are you in your right mind?"

Hameed rose and walked fast into the ballroom. But it was too early; the music had not yet started. He fumed inwardly at Rekha for her cold, uncooperative behaviour. Now might be a good moment, he thought, to disclose to her that it had actually been him on the phone, impersonating Faridi, and summoning her here to waste her time. He knew Rekha would see red when she found out the truth.

He returned to the dining hall. Rekha was just about to rise and go.

"So you won't be my partner for the dance?"

Rekha got up to leave, without answering.

"Then why do you think I called you here?"

Rekha glowered at him darkly. "What's that supposed to mean?"

"You think I don't know how to mimic the Colonel's voice?"

"Oh, may God rot your soul in hell!" She flopped back onto her chair.

"How content I would be if you always spoke to me in those tones! You don't even know how the universe of my heart contracts and expands when you purse your lips in displeasure."

"You're such an idiot. Go to hell," said Rekha, on the verge of tears.

"It would be enough for me if you let me live as *your* idiot," Hameed said, in a mock tragic voice.

Rekha just chewed her lower lip in angry despair.

"It wouldn't hurt you to occasionally smile when you looked at me."

"You have wasted my time," Rekha said through clenched teeth.

"And you seem hell-bent on laying waste to *me*." Hameed again sighed a deep sigh.

"Chirp away, little parrot."

"But you can't leave."

"No, I won't. And I have an idea that something *is* going to happen here tonight."

"That is to say...?"

"You wait and see. Perhaps I'll be your dancing partner after all."

Hameed fell silent. He was a bit worried that Rekha might have a plan to do something drastic to get back at him—as she had done at the High Circle Nightclub not long ago.*

Rekha burst out laughing. "So? You gave up the ghost when I called your bluff?"

"If you'll promise to always laugh just like that, I'll promise to cut off my head and donate it to the National Museum."

"But who is that girl?" Rekha asked, looking toward Shaheena.

"Her name is Shaheena. Her mother is Begum Irshad."

"Ah, yes. Isn't she the one who won last year's singles title at badminton?"

"The very same."

"But why were you surprised to see her with Anwar?"

"Nothing special, except that Anwar doesn't come from the same class."

"Then again, you don't come from Colonel Faridi's class, either."

---

* In #62, *The Laughing Corpse.* – Ed.

"Colonel Faridi doesn't belong to any class. If you were to try to find some class to fit him in, you'd fail—such a class hasn't come into existence yet."

Though he was talking to Rekha, Hameed's eyes were on Shaheena. Anwar had been casting sidelong glances at Hameed, but he wasn't really trying to get Hameed's attention. Hameed didn't look towards him, either.

"You have eyes for no one but her," Rekha observed.

"Yes, because I'm damned mad at her. What the hell does she mean by showing off her midriff like that? How utterly vulgar! Women who wear such blouses revolt me. Imagine if I were to show up here clad in nothing but bathing trunks. Why, the whole city would be in an uproar! Anyway, jokes aside, I think the belly is the ugliest part of the human anatomy. I mean that seriously."

"You're babbling your usual nonsense. Is that a brain you've got, or a road roller?"

Hameed's attention was still fixed on Shaheena. A coffee set had been served at her table, along with plates full of snacks. She and Anwar were drinking the coffee, but it was clear from Shaheena's body language that she was in a fair temper. She was too far away for Hameed to hear her words, but her lips were moving fast. Her eyes seemed to contract at times and open wide at others. Anwar was looking at her with an expression of dismay and disbelief.

Then a loud *thwack!* resounded throughout the hall. Hameed blinked involuntarily, for the source of the sound was a slap that had been delivered with full-blooded force to Anwar's face.

Anwar sprang up from his chair, but it seemed his astonishment had locked his legs, for he stood there unmoving.

Shaheena was screaming at the top of her lungs. "You

bastard! Son of a swine! Yes, I have five hundred and fifty-five husbands. What's it to you, you dirty dog?"

Then she began tearing at her clothes. Pandemonium ensued. Quickly, tables began to empty as guests left their chairs and crowded around the couple. Shaheena was still loudly proclaiming herself to be the wife of five hundred and fifty-five husbands.

Hameed pushed through the press of bodies, caught hold of Anwar by the arm, and pulled him out.

"What's going on here?" he asked Anwar.

"I have no idea," Anwar responded calmly. "I don't understand it myself." He spoke as if he was just a casual spectator; he didn't seem particularly bothered by the incident. In the meantime, Shaheena had overturned a table, scattering its contents. Then she began to pick up various pieces of crockery and silverware and break them, or throw them at people. The crowd withdrew in a hurry, the way a film of algae over stagnant water breaks up when a stone is chucked in.

"Hey, she doesn't seem to be in her right mind. You gave her too much to drink, maybe?"

"No." Anwar finally seemed to be getting a little concerned. "But is she planning to strip naked, now? I should hope not."

Shaheena began to leap and prance about like a savage. Her hair was disheveled, and there was no clothing left on her body, save for her bra and petticoat.

3

Hameed and Rekha

The Manager of the Arlecchino entered the hall at a run; he was at his wit's end. Hameed caught him by the hand.

"She's suffered a fit of some sort," Hameed said.

"Yes, yes. It seems so. So what should I do now?"

"Have her transferred to a vacant room immediately. Otherwise this might affect your business."

"You're right!" exclaimed the Manager, and raced off to the front desk.

Shaheena had thrown herself upon the floor, where she was snarling and roaring like a wild animal.

"Move! Please move away from here!" Hameed shouted at the top of his voice. But no one was listening. In fact, some of those present began to jeer and pass snide remarks at him, unaware that he was an officer of the Criminal Investigation Department. His ID wasn't inscribed on his face, after all. There might have been a couple of his acquaintances in the crowd, but none who were paying attention.

Finally, Hameed got on the hotel's P.A. system. "LADIES AND GENTLEMEN! PLEASE MOVE AWAY FROM THE PATIENT. SHE'S SUFFERING A NERVOUS BREAKDOWN, SOME KIND OF A FIT," he announced in a loud, commanding voice. "THANK YOU... BUT THERE'S

STILL A THICK CROWD OF PEOPLE THERE TO THE LEFT... PLEASE, YOU TOO, MOVE ASIDE."

By the time Hameed succeeded in dispersing the crowd, three duty constables had come in from the street outside. Shaheena was lying rigid on the floor. Rekha found Shaheena's sari and used it to cover her body. A stretcher was procured, and Shaheena was wheeled to a vacant room under the Manager's supervision. She was still unconscious. A doctor had been summoned. Now only Hameed, Rekha, and Anwar were left in the room with her.

Hameed stared hard at Anwar. "What was that she was saying about five hundred and fifty-five husbands?" he asked.

"I don't know."

"What was she saying before she slapped you?"

"I don't remember the words; she just started ranting and raving."

"Have you two been friends for long?"

"I don't remember."

"Anwar, are your feet still here on earth?"

"Yes," he answered nonchalantly, and turned his attention back to Shaheena.

"Rekha, look in the phone book, find the number, and call Begum Irshad," said Hameed.

"You can't do that," Anwar said, without bothering to turn towards Hameed.

"Excuse me, I am the officer of the law in charge here. Rekha, go ahead and call Begum Irshad."

"You'll pay a heavy price for this," Anwar muttered.

Hameed gestured toward the door. "Get. Out."

"Well you're flying high, aren't you!" Anwar said, looking Hameed over from head to foot.

"I am placing you under arrest," Hameed snarled. "You

are a drug dealer, and you passed her a charas cigarette to smoke."

Anwar smiled and offered a correction. "It was bhang, actually!"

"Ask the duty constables to come in," Hameed told Rekha. She went out immediately.

"Why are you so bent on your own ruination?" Anwar glared at Hameed.

"Shut up."

Anwar sighed deeply. Then he said, "All right. Maybe you'll even succeed in taking me to the police lock-up. But later..."

The door opened before he could finish his sentence. The constables entered and saluted Hameed.

"Keep this man in your custody," he said, with a gesture toward Anwar.

"Please come with us." A constable made a move to catch Anwar by his arm. But they were interrupted. The door opened suddenly with a bang, as if it were the proverbial bull making a forced entry into the china shop. The newcomer was Begum Irshad. She seemed utterly distraught, and fell upon Shaheena with the cry, "My daughter! Oh my daughter!"

"Madam, please restrain yourself," Hameed said to her firmly.

She turned to Hameed and screamed furiously, "Are you Anwar, the crime reporter?"

"No. I am Captain Hameed from the Intelligence Bureau."

Begum Irshad looked deflated, almost fearful. "Oh, no! No!" she cried.

Hameed pointed to Anwar. "This here would be Anwar, the crime reporter."

Begum Irshad gritted her teeth and hissed, "You! You're the one ruining my daughter's life!"

"Madam, that's news to me," Anwar smiled. "You don't even know me."

"You're turning her into a drug addict!"

"And how did you come to learn of this, ma'am?" Anwar's tone was sarcastic.

"Never mind how I got to know. If you don't stop harassing Shaheena, I'll take very strong action against you."

Anwar shrugged off the threat, and made no reply, but Hameed intervened quickly.

"Yes, Begum Irshad, he most surely deserves it. I'm placing this man under arrest on a charge of drug peddling. He's been found in possession of a twenty-gram packet of cocaine!" He turned to a policeman. "Take him away."

Anwar followed the constables without a word. Begum Irshad said to Hameed, "Sir, I am grateful to you for your assistance. Now I want to take my daughter home. Will you help me do this, too?"

"Yes, of course."

"I'll be forever indebted to you."

"And what action would you suggest be taken against Mr. Anwar?"

"Oh, nothing... I just want him to stop meeting with my little girl."

"Rest assured. I will make that absolutely clear to him. I've had a doctor summoned to see your daughter."

"There's no need for that, Captain Hameed," she said slowly. "It's not a disease or anything like that. I can declare with full conviction that Anwar, that swine, has given her some sort of intoxicating substance."

"Maybe. Do you have your car?"

"Yes. My car is right outside."

"Fine," Hameed said, "Miss Rekha Larson, please

assist Begum Irshad in conveying her daughter to her car."

With that, Rekha and Begum Irshad put Shaheena on the stretcher, and two constables helped them bring her to the car. Hameed and Rekha came back to the hotel room to wait for the physician, whose fees had already been paid by Begum Irshad. Hameed summoned the constables and Anwar, and told the constables to go. "Everything's okay here," he said.

The constables looked from Anwar to Hameed with questioning eyes. Hameed reassured them, "I'll take care of it. You can go."

"So? Lost your nerve or something?" Anwar asked Hameed with a vitriolic smile.

"Yes, that's right, I did. Now you go make yourself scarce too."

"My name is Anwar, dear honorary Captain."

"Did I say it was Chanchala Devi, you stray cur?"

"Now go tear your hair out," Anwar said, rising. "I'm off."

Rekha had been watching the exchange with wonder. After Anwar's departure, she said, "You've been acting strangely, right from the very beginning of all this."

"Forget it, it's not important. As I was saying…"

Before he could complete the sentence, the Manager barged in and exclaimed in an injured voice, "Dear Captain, may I know what's been going on here, and why?"

"Please take a chair. It's difficult to come to a conclusion, yet…"

"I fear she was high on bhang," the Manager said hurriedly.

"Very possibly."

"Oh, the Arlecchino's reputation is going down the tubes!" the Manager said in a voice heavy with worry.

"Day in and day out, the children of the rich and the powerful come here to brawl and scuffle like street gangsters. Just a few days ago there was a young man from a very prominent family dining here, who hurled a plate full of food at another prominent person. Worse still, a girl was kidnapped!"

"Yes, very bad for business, certainly."

"Then tell me, what should I do? If things go on like this much longer, the only clientele this hotel will have left will be a crowd of brainless idiots."

"You should get a notice posted on the main door, to the effect that women under the influence of cannabis are kindly requested not to enter."

The Manager smiled obligingly. "The upper class youth are becoming morally and ethically bankrupt. Anyone can see that."

"Certainly. Then why don't you open a school of morals and ethics on the premises?"

"Captain, sir, it's with the utmost seriousness that I am seeking your advice."

"And it's with the utmost seriousness that I am advising you to organize the sale of bhang in your bar, alongside the sale of spirits and liqueurs. Obviously, in such a situation, noisy and embarrassing scenes like this will become common, and no longer worthy of special note. For I doubt there is any way you can prevent women who are high on bhang from coming here."

The Manager had nothing to say to this. After a moment or two of polite silence, he left.

Rekha smiled, "You really are behaving strangely today."

"And you know what? Girls are ready to do anything for a man who behaves strangely. Ha ha, it's a strange quirk of nature, that! You may ask them, 'Why are you so hopelessly enamoured with that fellow?' and they'll

answer in all sincerity, 'Oh, he is always so lost in himself—it's so romantic!' But if by any chance they end up
with a *husband* who is always lost in himself, then that
same fellow will be described as a perfect fool—worse than
a fool. They won't say he's different or unique or romantic
anymore, oh no; they'll call him cracked and egocentric."

"Who asked you to jabber away like this?"

"Ah, Rekha... never mind my jabber. What I really
want to tell you is that the vision of your rose-petal lips is
forever dancing round and round in my head. When you
flutter those long lashes of yours..."

"Shut up," Rekha cut him short.

"Oh, Rekha, please get up. The music for the next
number has started. Such opportunities don't come
often. Outside in the open, the moonlight will have spread
over everything like a white sheet; there will be a pleasant
breeze, and the moon... the young moon will be playing
hide and seek with her dear father, there behind the
clouds. *Uttho wagarna hash'r naheen ho ga phir kabhie...*
Rise, oh rise now, for doomsday will only come once!"

"I'm sleepy. I think I'll go home now. No, wait. What's
the story with Shaheena? At first you were livid with
Anwar, but then you let him off so easily."

"Oh, I just have these changes of mood, you know,"
said Hameed airily.

"But what was the need to tell Begum Irshad that
you'd found cocaine in his possession?"

"What harm did it do me? I was just wagging my
tongue."

"But she took it to be the truth!"

"Yes. And in spite of that, all she asked was that Anwar
be prevented from seeing her daughter. She didn't seem
the least bit interested in having any criminal proceedings initiated against him."

"I agree, her reaction was strange."

"Strange or not, I am not prepared to worry my head about it. You shouldn't tire yourself out either, pondering over such matters needlessly."

Before Rekha could reply, one of the bellboys came up to say that the Captain was wanted on the phone in the Manager's office.

"Okay, I'm coming," said Hameed, and went to the Manager's office. The Manager wasn't there, having apparently left to give Hameed some privacy.

"Hello."

"Hameed?" It was Faridi speaking.

"Yes, sir."

"Good. You've handled the situation there in a satisfactory manner."

"But how did you know?" Hameed was surprised.

"There's no need to ask such stupid questions."

"So you've got your secret network of spies spread out through the city once again?"

"Now listen. Stop pestering Inspector Rekha. The girl whom you were detailed to watch is currently in the ballroom of the Maypole, along with a companion—an Austrian. The man I have watching her is not up to the job of dealing with what I expect may happen."

"And so you want me to go there pronto, even if I have to walk on my head to do it," Hameed said with a trace of bitterness in his voice.

"Please don't do any such thing. You are authorized to take a cab."

"Well, I wouldn't have used a helicopter. But what do I do with Rekha?"

"What, is she tied to your coat-tails?" Faridi's voice was angry and unpleasant.

"What do I have to do once I reach Maypole?"

"You have to watch the girl. That's all."

"Oh God!" Hameed said in a voice choked with emotion.

"I can keep watch over a water buffalo from a distance, but I can't keep watch over a girl from a distance—not again. You can only imagine how hard it's become. How can I explain it to my poor heart? But anyway, my heart doesn't understand a word of Urdu these days."

"Stop blabbering. There's no need to watch from a distance. You can even chat her up if you like; and there's no need to conceal your name and address from her."

"Ah! In that case, may God grant you even greater blessings and higher ranks..." Hameed began effusively, but the connection had been broken at the other end. Hameed returned to the dining hall. Rekha was still there.

"Sorry, I have to leave immediately," Hameed told Rekha. "My nephew's wife's brother-in-law just died. I have to be there in ten minutes."

"Oh, wasn't he the one who lived in... er, over there?"

"Yes, yes, that's the one. I have to go now."

"Then I'll come with you. I knew the deceased well."

"No, no, this was somebody else. You didn't know him at all."

"I knew him very well. In fact, we worked together just a year ago."

"Impossible. He never held a job."

"He must have kept it a secret from you. I'll come with you. I must!"

Hameed was stymied. *What a bother!*

"I can't let you go anywhere by yourself today," Rekha went on. "Your stars are unfavourable."

"My stars are fine. I know more astrology than you!"

"Oh, to hell with astrology then. But I really must go with you. Otherwise, I'm warning you... you had better get ready for another storm, right here, one that you won't be able to free yourself from."

"Oh dear God!" Hameed exclaimed, and almost fell

back in his chair. "Please, listen. That was the Colonel on the phone. He's sending me somewhere on duty."

"Whatever. I'm still not going to let you go alone."

"You're not?" Hameed said.

"No. Not a chance."

"Right. Then please give me just a couple of minutes."

Hameed tried to get up, but Rekha caught him by the sleeve and said softly: "What's the use? I'll have my hands on the lapels of your coat, in front of everybody, within no time."

"Death take me now," Hameed mumbled in a choked voice. Then he suddenly changed his tone and spoke sharply. "If I'm late in reporting there, you'll be answerable to the Colonel."

"Not to worry. I will answer to him."

Hameed breathed a sigh of defeat and said, "All right, as you wish."

They came out. "I have a car," Rekha said.

"What's that? *You* have a car?" Hameed exclaimed.

"It's my brother's."

"Your brother's? And here I believed you were all alone in this world! That's the only reason my heart went out to you. Fine then: now we part. You go your way, and I'll go mine."

"Starting tomorrow. Today we take the same road."

"Father Hardstone will pound my head to pieces. He very clearly said 'Don't take Rekha with you'."

"Sorry, what was that? I can't hear you." Rekha unlocked her car and slid into the driver's seat. "Come, sit in front."

"No, I'm okay back here," Hameed said, flopping down in the back seat.

"Where to?" asked Rekha.

"Arjun Pura," Hameed exhaled.

The Prick Of A Needle

The moment the car entered Park Lane, Hameed was determined to escape. Traffic was heavy; Rekha was obliged to reduce her speed and concentrate hard on the road. Hameed opened the back door gently, slid silently out of the car, and walked at a fast clip into the adjoining alley. By the time he'd walked a hundred yards, he was quite out of breath, and feeling a bit nauseous. In any event, he was happy to be free of Rekha. After all, he had Faridi's permission to chat up the girl at the Maypole; how could poor old Rekha compete with a new face?

Coming out at the other end of the alley, he hailed a cab and asked the driver to take him to the Maypole, quick. By now the problem of Shaheena and Anwar had slipped from his mind completely; all his thoughts were on the girl he had been ordered to keep a watch on by making her acquaintance.

He paid the taxi driver and entered the main restaurant of the hotel. The restaurant was very nearly deserted at that hour, but the sound of music could be heard coming from the recreation hall. He paid for a temporary membership card and entered the ballroom, which was packed—the ambience like a storm of lights and colours and scents. It would not be easy to locate the girl in this crowd.

While it seemed doubtful that he would be able to find the girl quickly, he was delighted to see Qasim in the ballroom—Qasim, the gigantic fool, who was a perennial source of entertainment for Hameed.* He was sitting in the left aisle, watching the dancers with his mouth hanging open, as if it was his first time in a ballroom. Hameed approached quietly; Qasim was so absorbed in watching the spectacle that he didn't realize who was behind him.

"Having fun tonight, aren't we?" Hameed whispered in his ear.

"Yup!" Qasim replied without looking. Then he suddenly turned to look at the newcomer. "What... who?" he spluttered. "You! Pf-please go. Go away, pf-peremptorily."

"You mean 'promptly', I think. But why are you acting so incensed, dear brother?"

"You dirty dog! You've been feeding poisonous lies to my wife!"

"What's that?"'

"You told her that her husband Qasim speaks ill of her to his friends."

"Oh no, not at all. Not of her... of your father."

"What...? What did you say?"

"Just this, that you speak ill of your father among your friends."

"You lie, you tripster! I mean trickster!"

"Well, what do I know about it? Your wife was the one who told me."

---

* Qasim first appears in *Jasusi Dunya* #33, *Burf kay Booth* ("The Snow Ghosts"). He is a very tall and very fat young man with a childish and unpredictable nature and an unusual sort of speech impediment. Qasim has had an arranged marriage to his first cousin, with whom he is constantly feuding; they live with his stern father, the textile baron Khan Bahadur Asim. – Ed.

"She talks dribble, er, drivel. How could you believe her?"

"I won't, then," Hameed said, and this seemed to make Qasim quite happy, as though some major issue had been resolved. He turned back to watch the show, his mouth hanging open as usual; a supple young girl's dancing had caught his attention.

"Qasim, have you ever tried dancing?" Hameed asked.

"Man it, I can't damage... I mean damn it, can't manage. Don't have the sprills. Skills."

"If at first you don't succeed, try, try again!"

"The hell with you, go on! And with whom would I dance? Curse this enormous b-b-body of mine, yes, curse it to hell!"

"But I can teach you."

"Oh, do teach me, my dear b-brother. I'll be grateful to you for the rest of my life."

"But you must look for the right girl to be your partner."

"Where? Where should I look?" Qasim wailed like a helpless orphan.

"Choose anyone from this big crowd. Then I'll clinch the deal for you. What about that slim one over there?"

"Ah... ha ha. Really?" Qasim laughed out loud, his huge mouth open like a dark cave.

By a stroke of luck, Hameed had sighted the very girl that Faridi had ordered him to watch. She was dancing with a middle-aged man.

"There... How about that girl right over there, the one in the blue skirt?"

"Wow! I swear to God, my dear brother Ghameed, she's real eye-mehndi... I mean eye-candy."

"Good. So what's your plan?"

"What can I say? You thing of somethink... er, think of something." Qasim's voice was quivering with excitement.

"Okay, so listen. As soon as this round finishes, you

go after her and keep asking her for the next dance. I think she will finally accept."

"B-b-but brother Ghameed, I don't even know how to prance... er, dance." Qasim gulped hard. The mere thought of dancing had already made him go pale.

"Oh, don't you worry about it. Girls always know how to lead. Ninety percent of men don't know how to dance, but they dance anyway. You just keep stepping, and everything will be fine."

"Okay..." Qasim was panting steadily now. "But what am I going to say to her?"

"Just say 'May I request the next dance...?' That should be enough. Even if she tries to refuse on pretext of tiredness or something, you just keep repeating the request."

"But brother... I think she's a forgerer. I mean a foreigner."

"Don't be afraid. Go try. If it turns out that she doesn't like you, I'll come give you a rebuke and shoo you away."

"You? Rebuke me?" Qasim growled.

"My dear simple friend," Hameed said with some irritation, "try to understand the subtlety of things. What I mean is, I'll come and reprimand you, and then you should quietly slink off."

"No. Not a chance. You're just trying to p-p-play some trick on me."

"No trick, my dear friend. If she won't accept your request for the next dance, it's certain that her older sister over there will. There, look, that hefty lady... the one in the dark green skirt."

"W-where, where?" Qasim asked excitedly.

"See over there. She's dancing with that scrawny fellow who looks like a chicken."

Qasim looked, and then braced himself as his body

did some strange contortions. He ran his tongue over his lips eagerly.

"Ample and substantial, is she not?" Hameed asked Qasim.

"By God! She's just the thing. She's made for me." Qasim was bubbling with joy, his eyes following the voluptuous lady, who was dancing with a reed-thin man. Hameed, of course, had other designs.

"So. You just keep asking that first girl for a dance, no matter what she says," Hameed said.

"And what happens then?" Qasim asked with interest.

"I'll give you a harsh rebuke and make you scurry off."

"No, no. There's some trick to it."

"That big girl isn't going to pay you any attention unless I treat you harshly."

"My dear big brother, don't make a p-pf-fool of me!"

"Okay, fine. Let it go. I'll dance with both of them myself, one after the other."

"But... but I don't understand at all what you mean!"

"Look, brother Qasim, what I mean to say is this: the two girls are sisters, but there's rivalry between them. So, when I chase you away with a flea in your ear after your request to the smaller one, the other, the bigger one, will naturally be more inclined to favour you. Do you get it now?"

"Got it." Qasim nodded gravely. "She'll want to outdo her shickster, and therefore, she will agree to be my pf-partner."

"Quite right, quite right. Thank God, you've got it at last. But my friend, you seem to be acting somewhat sad and downcast these days. What's the matter?"

"Dear brother Hameed," Qasim said, blowing a blast of warm air. "Don't ask. It's become clear to me that the b-b-bitch will not stop until I'm dead."

"Which bitch? None of the bitches I know are so pow-erful, I think."

"You don't understand. It's that mule bitch I'm spf-speaking of, the one the world calls my wife."

"Why? Some new development?"

"Yes," Qasim said, in voice choked with emotion. "She has adopted the young child of one of the servants; she has him calling me Daddy. Just imagine, dear brother, how pf-p-painful it is!"

"What's your problem? Let her go ahead."

"She makes pf-fun of me, that ulloo ki patthi."

"Perhaps you should call her 'uncle ki patthi', instead of 'ulloo ki patthi'," Hameed suggested.

"Uncle-nuncle, that blasted fellow! Why did he have to go and tie a moush hash—a housh maish—I mean, a house mouse, to the coat-tails of an elephant?"

"Vah vah, Qasim, you are fast becoming a poet!"

"Dear brother Hameed, to hell with p-poetry, and to hell with my own life! Do you know, she now has an aunt of hers as a permanent house guest? That b-b-blasted b-bitch. Several times a day I pf-feel like shooting her aunt to death."

"How old is this aunt of hers?"

"Oh hell, she must be some age or the other, who cares?"

"I mean, is she an old hag?"

"W-what? Why do you want to kn-kn-kn-know?" Qasim scowled.

"Oh, no reason. No reason at all," Hameed said. "Look, the round has ended, the music has stopped. Now come. Come with me."

They practically lunged toward the bar, for that was where the girl seemed to be headed. Hameed assumed that she meant to stay and drink at the bar for a while. But he got an unpleasant surprise; he saw the girl lean her elbows on the bar counter, bend towards the bartender, say something to him, and then turn around and head straight for the exit. All of this happened so quickly that Hameed had to give up on the idea of following her. He took a few idle steps in the direction of the dining hall. Meanwhile, Qasim was whispering loudly in his ear.

"She's left! She's gone! She's turned... She's stopped... Oh God, she's left! She's gone away, dear brother Hameed, what will we do now?"

"I'll be beaten like an omelette!" Hameed said, turning towards Qasim; for some reason, he felt terribly irked with him suddenly.

"But... Her older shickster..." The words got trapped in Qasim's voice box.

"Oh, to hell with her!" Hameed spoke in a stage whisper. He was truly angry now.

"How's that, dear brother?" asked Qasim. Hameed waved him away irritably, but Qasim would not give up. "Of course, to hell with the one who went away. But her poor older shickster is bf-b-b-blameless, isn't she?"

Hameed said nothing; Qasim pulled him back into the ballroom, towards the table they had been occupying a few minutes before.

"Come, sit, dear brother. I swear there are times when I feel full of love for you."

"Yes, I suppose anything is possible," Hameed nodded in agreement. Now he was regretting that he hadn't followed the girl. It must have been important to keep her under observation; why else would the Colonel have directed him there?

"Oh... Ah, my dear brother Ghameed!" Suddenly Qasim was speaking in a choked voice. "Look—just look over there!"

"What is it now?" Hameed asked irritably. But his irritation evaporated as soon as he turned to look in the direction Qasim was pointing. For the girl had reentered the ballroom, accompanied this time by a man.

"Come! Let's make our ap-p-pf-proach!" Qasim said, shaking Hameed by the shoulder.

"It's no good, dear boy. She's no longer alone," Hameed said.

"So what? If the bastard objects, I'll nake his breck," Qasim said furiously.

Hameed had no ready answer. His brains felt snowed in and he couldn't seem to think right. His plan had gone awry.

The music for the next dance was starting up, and the girl's companion stayed at her table. Hameed had assumed that the girl was there alone; though Faridi had said there would be an Austrian man with her, he hadn't noticed any foreign-looking companion. Hameed's plan had been to set Qasim loose on her, then go and chase him away, after which the girl was sure to be thankful and act friendly with him; that way he could strike up an acquaintance with her, just as Faridi had ordered. That was why he'd been breaking his head this whole time, trying to get Qasim to cooperate.

But now that it was clear that the girl wasn't alone, the original plan was no longer feasible. Hameed felt a surge of hostility towards the girl's companion. He didn't appear to be a foreigner, so his role in the scheme of things was obscure. He was a healthy young man of thirty or thirty-five; handsome, but with a hard-boiled look about him—the set of his mouth and eyes hinted at a cruel streak in his personality.

The music commenced. Hameed and Qasim stayed put. Qasim was still muttering, "How sad, her older shickster... there she goes... going... gone!" Hameed saw that the ample-and-substantial woman in the green skirt was dancing with someone new. Qasim was wringing his hands.

"My dear pf-friend and brother, sometimes you really do break my heart," he said in a bitter, disappointed voice.

"It's your own bad luck. I can't fight it for you."

"You're right, there's nothing left for you to do. I will take matters into my own hands."

"What will you do?"

"I'll set p-pf-fire to my house."

"Oh, enough! Have you totally forgotten the lash of Khan Bahadur Saheb's whip?"

Qasim gritted his teeth in silent rage. The next dance had started. Hameed had been taking an occasional nonchalant look over at the girl in the aisle on the far side of the hall. He looked again now, and it seemed that suddenly she was alone. Hameed rose from his chair so he could see clearly; there was no one else at the girl's table. He had a view of the entire aisle now.

Drawing a deep breath, Hameed started walking toward the far aisle; Qasim called after him repeatedly, but Hameed paid no heed. He reached the aisle and stood quietly near the girl. It seemed to him that she was anxious about something. Hameed looked around on all sides, but her companion was nowhere to be seen.

The girl, now clearly frightened, was casting nervous glances all around her. In the process, her eyes fleetingly met Hameed's, but she showed no particular interest and looked away. Nevertheless, Hameed walked up to her table and said, "Could I have the next dance?"

"I'm sorry?" She flinched, then gave a faint, colourless smile. "I'm afraid I'm rather exhausted right now."

"Exhaustion is our constant companion in life," Hameed said philosophically. "Anyway, I have no choice now but to commit suicide."

The girl made no obvious reaction to this, but Hameed

felt that she was looking at him suspiciously. Her face, already pale, now seemed even paler. Hameed pulled up a chair and asked, as he proceeded to sit in it, "Is there something upsetting you?"

"No, not at all. Why would you think that?" Now she seemed more surprised than afraid.

"You *are* afraid of something!"

"What if I am? And how dare you speak to me—I'm not some streetwalker, okay?"

Hameed, leaning against the back of the chair, smiled and said:

"And I'm no rogue myself. I'm a gentleman."

The girl stared hard at him for a long minute. Hameed's smile didn't slip for an instant. Suddenly, she bent toward him and spoke softly, with her elbows planted on the table.

"You think you can terrorize me? Not at all. Just try it and see. I have many friends right here in this ballroom who will come to my aid."

"I think you misunderstand me."

"Did I invite you to my table?" she demanded furiously.

"No, of course not."

"Then what's the idea?"

"There is no particular idea. It's just that your stars and mine seem to be aligned at the moment."

The girl opened her mouth to respond, but then she leaned back and looked toward the main door of the ballroom. Involuntarily, Hameed turned to look too. But at the same moment, he felt a sharp prick in his right arm—someone had stuck a needle into him, right through his jacket. He drew a gasping breath, and then exhaled with a hiss. He held the arm tightly with his left hand and turned toward the girl. She pushed her chair back with a hurried movement, as if it was she who had pricked him.

Hameed felt that his whole body was being invaded by

waves of heat. The site of the needle-prick was throbbing like a boil filled with pus and about to burst. The girl rose to go, but Hameed couldn't even open his mouth to speak. As he watched her leave, he felt himself go rigid, his muscles incapable of movement. The noise of the orchestra was like the cacophony of a fish market. He made another unsuccessful attempt to rise. His whole body broke out in a cold sweat. His powers of thought and comprehension were intact, but he was unable to use his muscles.

Slowly, strength returned to the muscles of his face and neck. He looked around, hoping that Qasim would still be there. Relief ran through his body when he found Qasim where he had left him. With great difficulty, he nodded his head towards him again and again, hoping to catch his eye. Finally, Qasim noticed him and came over.

"Qasim, please take me home," Hameed said, almost in a whisper. "I swear I can't move under my own power. You'll have to carry me to your car."

Qasim laughed his inane laugh. "Oh, no. How could that be? You're joking, dear b-b-brother Ghameed."

"I mean it." Hameed wetted his dry lips with an effort. "Quickly, please, Qasim. Take me home right away. Or else phone the Colonel and tell *him* to come get me."

5

A Dangerous Gift

Rasheeda Khan placed the morning newspaper on the tea tray and brought it to Anwar. While she was still pouring the tea, Anwar demanded that she read him the newspaper. At this, she lost her temper.

"Are you bloody blind?"

"Yes, I am blind. That's why I need you to read today's news to me."

"What am I, your servant?"

"A very old question, which I never answer."

Rasheeda glared. "What happened last night?"

"Nothing much. Don't pry into matters that don't concern you personally."

"Did you see the editorial in *The Observer* today?"

"I don't have time to waste reading that nonsense."

"That's for the best. Because if you *had* read it, you'd probably be lacing your tea with arsenic instead of sugar."

"What's that?"

"Who was that girl you got drunk with last night at the Arlecchino?"

"*The Observer* has something to say about it, does it?"

Rasheeda picked up the paper and read. "'*The Crimes of A Crime Reporter:* A well-known crime reporter for a local newspaper was seen last night dancing in a four-star hotel while naked and drunk. This crime reporter is rumoured to be friendly with a few senior officers of the police; this may be the reason he does not seem to recognize any moral restrictions on his own public behaviour. If an ordinary person had acted the same way, they would have undoubtedly landed in the police lock-up straight away. But clearly, this crime reporter's relations with the defenders of the law have proved useful to him. Had the same incident occurred in any civilized country—'"

Anwar raised his hand, "Okay. That's enough."

"So it's a fact," Rasheeda said. Without waiting for a response, she went on, "And who was this girl, the one from the 'wealthy business family'?"

"It was Shaheena. What do they say about her?"

"That she was dancing naked too, along with said Crime Reporter."

"Sure, and all while the editor of *The Observer* sat serenely in his office, playing the sarangi. Well, he'll get his come-uppance soon."

"But what really happened?"

"Shaheena suddenly had some kind of a fit, like a mental stroke, and started tearing off her clothes."

"And you? What happened to you?"

"I think I'm about to suffer a similar fit right now."

"Have no fear. It may be early morning, but I'm wearing my heavy-duty Bata sandals. Why did you take Shaheena there in the first place?"

"Because it's thanks to her that my creditors are loving me again."

"I see! You've taken on a case for her."

Anwar remained silent. Rasheeda gave him a dark look and said, "Why are you trying to hide all this from me?"

"Is there anything that ever stays hidden from you?"

Rasheeda was peeved. "Not that I really want to know."

"Thanks."

Anwar drank his tea, the paper open before him. He noticed an interesting news item in it. His own paper, *The New Star*, didn't have the story in question. The news story was as follows:

THE STRANGE EXPERIENCE OF CAPTAIN HAMEED, OFFICER OF THE C.I.D.

While in conversation with a foreign woman in the ballroom of the Maypole last night, the above-named officer claims to have had a strange experience. He reportedly felt something sharp prick his right arm; within seconds, his body became rigid, and he was unable to move a muscle. Captain Hameed says that his attention was distracted at the crucial moment, so he is not certain if the lady to whom he was speaking was responsible or not. The Captain was quickly rendered so immobile that he was not even able to speak; the lady then went away, leaving him in this condition. Having met her just a few minutes before the incident occurred, the Captain does not know her name. He says that soon after he felt the pricking sensation, his arm began to hurt very badly, as though from a major wound. Since he was unable to move, a friend had to carry him out of the ballroom and into a car. As he was being driven home in the friend's car, the gusts of cool night air seemed, surprisingly, to return him to normalcy. His body became alert and active as before, and the pain of the wound was reduced to nothing more than would be expected after the prick of a needle.

Medical reports indicate that some sharp object did indeed prick the Captain in the arm, but there were no traces of toxicity in the blood. The doctors say there is no evidence that he was injected with any drug or poison.

"What the hell! I wonder what *that* was all about?" Anwar mumbled.

"What?" Rasheeda said.

Anwar passed the paper to her. She read the news

item, and said, "What was the use, or the point, of printing this?"

"Don't you think it's interesting?"

"But I thought he was at the Arlecchino. This story is about something that happened in the Maypole."

Before Anwar could reply, the phone rang. He picked up the receiver. A woman spoke.

"Anwar?"

"Who is it?"

"It's Shaheena."

"Shaheena! I hope you're properly clothed?"

"Anwar, for God's sake, don't make fun of me! Oh, I'm so ashamed, I don't think you'll ever see me go out again."

"I wonder..."

"Anwar, I beseech you! Please listen. I've never had any sort of fit or seizure before in my life. I'm definitely not a mental patient."

"The Manager of the Arlecchino thinks that you were high on bhang."

"That's rubbish. My only addiction is to cigarettes."

"Well, what is it that you want now?"

"I am convinced that my mother is in some serious trouble. She's opening up a bit, but only to forbid me from ever seeing you again. She believes that yesterday's incident was the work of the dangerous man who is the cause of her troubles. Apparently, he told her this himself. He also said that if anyone from our house made any attempt to contact the police, or even a private detective, they would be subjected to similar humiliation."

"I see. But your mother isn't prepared to disclose anything more about her troubles to you?"

"No, nothing. She just says I have to keep silent if I don't want her to lose her life."

"That's too bad. So what do you want me to do now?"

"The same thing I asked you to do when I met you."

"In spite of your mother's warning?"

"Can't you proceed in secret?"

"I can, but it'll cost more." Anwar winked at Rasheeda, but she curled her lips in distaste and said nothing.

"Don't worry about the cost," came the voice from the other end. "Are you coming to my birthday party today?"

"Well, I can. I'll come in disguise—but then how will you know me?"

"You'll be the one whose face I won't recognize."

"You mean everyone else there will be known to you personally?"

"Yes."

"Then won't your mother know all your friends, too?"

"No, there are quite a few she doesn't know."

"That's it, then. We're all set. I'll be there."

"In particular, I want you to see those two asses, so you'll know them."

"You mean the Dunkitales? Senior and Junior?"

"Yes, those fellows. It's very possible that they're the ones responsible for my mother's troubles."

"Okay, anything else?"

"Nothing else. Just please be here this evening. That's all."

Anwar put the receiver back in its cradle. He smiled at Rasheeda and winked.

"Did you hear that?" He spoke loudly, as if Rasheeda was hard of hearing. "On the conclusion of this case, I think I'll buy a fancy car."

"You've promised to buy a fancy car on the conclusion of many cases."

"This time I'll do it."

"We'll see."

Anwar finished his breakfast and rose. Rasheeda didn't move. She seemed upset with Anwar for some reason.

• • •

As promised, Anwar arrived at Irshad Manzil in the evening, disguised as a Eurasian. There was a lavish spread laid out. Nearly half the guests had arrived. Anwar looked all around for Shaheena but could not find her. He was a bit worried that someone might ask him who he was and what he was doing there, for no one in the crowd would recognize him in his disguise. He circulated through the hall as best he could, looking for Shaheena. Soon the hall became so crowded that it looked more like a political rally than a birthday celebration. *No one will bother to pay me any attention,* he thought.

Though he couldn't find Shaheena, he did find two people matching the descriptions of Dunkitale Senior and Dunkitale Junior. They were standing near a table laden with food and drink, having an argument about something. Anwar stood behind them, pretending to admire a painting that hung upon the wall. The old man looked well-preserved and physically strong. He sported a reddish beard. The son resembled the father so closely that except for the beard, it would have been difficult to tell them apart. The father was saying something.

"If I've said it once, I've said it a thousand times. Why do you babble so much when you don't have a grain of grey matter in your head?"

The son made a sour face. "I've got more brains than you, Pop. We can put it to a test whenever you feel like it."

"You're an ass."

"It's your blood running in my veins, Pop."

"What's that got to do with it? You can still be an ass, regardless."

The argument didn't proceed any further, because at that point Shaheena turned up. This evening, contrary to her usual style, she was dressed formally in a gharara. The younger Dunkitale made a strange sound, then cut it short, and said: "Pardon me, Miss Irshad, but I must tell you, you look very glamorous in that outfit! Doesn't she, Pop?"

"Yes, yes, absolutely." Dunkitale Senior nodded and smiled benevolently.

"Thank you." Shaheena smiled ravishingly, cast a casual glance at Anwar, and walked on to mingle with the other guests.

"Pop, that girl is going to make me dream all sorts of dreams."

"Eh? Yes, yes, it's quite possible." The old man sighed.

"Why the deep sigh, Pop?"

"Hunter, you stupid ass, I'll thrash you."

"Come out with it, tell me the truth. Do you like her too?"

"Hunter, please. Pack it in. I can lose my temper even at a glittering party like this."

"It's been a long time since you've lost your temper, Pop. Let's see you do it now!"

"No more gibberish," said the father, and moved off. But the son, Hunter, followed right behind him, so close that he seemed about to bump into him. Anwar left his place as well. Now he wanted to make contact with Shaheena, and this time he found her soon enough.

"Happy birthday, Miss Irshad. Many happy returns," he said.

"Thank you, thank you so much," Shaheena said, shaking Anwar's hand warmly. The two of them moved unobtrusively away to a spot where the crowd of people was comparatively thin.

"Good show," said Shaheena. "If you hadn't been the

only stranger here, I'd never have known it was you. Remarkable skill indeed. And you got very close to those two."

"Yes, I observed them closely. Both of them were gushing about how attractive you are."

"I really can't figure out what sort of father and son they are."

"I can't either. But it's early days yet."

"Right. I'm off to greet the other guests now."

"I'd like to inspect the place where your mother spoke with the stranger the other night."

"Go wherever you want. But what are you known as, in this place?"

"Joseph Peters."

"I'll have your name card put on the table for dinner."

"Hmm… yes, okay. But I'm not sure I'll stay till dinner."

"No, no, don't make that mistake. Our unknown enemy might notice you're missing. He's undoubtedly very clever—the incident at the Arlecchino proved that."

"You're right. Well, I guess I'll have to trust my instincts."

Shaheena went off to mingle with the other guests. Anwar moved aimlessly from table to table, looking at the trollies of drinks being pushed by the waiters. One of them stopped near him, but he only chose a soft drink. Anwar didn't drink, and even if he did, he wouldn't have had one here. He came face to face with Begum Irshad, and greeted and congratulated her like an old friend. Begum Irshad reciprocated effusively, not letting on at all that she didn't know him from Adam.

Afterwards, Anwar decided that rather than continue moving around unattached in that big crowd, he should join some group to remain inconspicuous. He went up to a group of young men who were sitting around a table with Hunter Dunkitale, making him the butt of their jokes. It seemed that his name was the current topic of ridicule, for Dunkitale was saying:

"No, not at all. You guys have it all wrong. Our name isn't spelled the same way as the words 'donkey' and 'tail'. Our name is spelled D-U-N-K-I-T-A-L-E. Got it?"

"Maybe so," someone said, "but if you write it in Urdu, it reads "donkeytail' all the same."

"Sorry, I can't help that." Hunter shook his head with regret.

"And what are your brothers called?" someone else asked.

"Sorry again. Pop married only once," Hunter said slowly. "So I have no siblings."

Everyone laughed out loud, and Hunter looked around at them blankly, apparently unaware that he himself had cracked a joke.

Another question was thrown at him. "And how old were you when you were born?"

"Wait a minute; let me go and ask Pop," he said, and went off, elbowing his way past the group.

Everybody laughed, but Anwar's eyes followed him. Instead of going toward his father, he went through one of the doors that led in to another part of the house. Roger Dunkitale, the father, was absorbed in a discussion with one of the city's leading businessmen. Anwar unobtrusively directed his steps toward the door through which Hunter had made his exit.

He was almost at the door when dinner was announced. The guests were requested to move to the adjoining hall where tables and places had been set. Anwar really didn't want to stay for dinner, so he walked quickly to the door Hunter had gone through, and opened it—to find himself in a corridor. He moved down the corridor, expecting to find a door leading out of the building into the grounds.

Doors lined both sides of the long corridor. One of them

opened suddenly, and someone came out so fast that he and Anwar collided. Anwar had to brace himself to avoid falling, and the person who had come out of the doorway dropped a large box that he was carrying. He bent quickly to pick it up. Anwar saw that it was Hunter Dunkitale. Picking up the box, he laughed an embarrassed laugh, as if he had been caught doing something wrong, or foolish.

"This... this is a birthday present for Miss Irshad," he said. He seemed a little out of breath.

"So what should I do about it?" Anwar glared at Hunter Dunkitale.

"Nothing... nothing special, but see, I'm a newcomer to your country. I don't really know anything about what sort of birthday presents the young women here prefer... Please, just have a look at it and tell me if it's suitable. Really, I'll be greatly obliged."

The moment he opened the box, Anwar flinched, swore, and jumped backward. A black snake, its hood spread wide, was looking Anwar in the eye, flicking its forked red tongue in and out. Anwar tightened his lips to a thin line and knit his brow. He looked about ready to launch a physical assault on Hunter.

6

The Crime, or the Criminal

Hunter Dunkitale guffawed, and kept on laughing.
"You want me to tell you if it's suitable?" Anwar
said through clenched teeth.

"Yes, I'd be very grateful. I'm not really sure if she'll
appreciate my gift."

Anwar took a step forward and grabbed Hunter by the
collar.

"What? What is this? Please!" Hunter jumped back in
confusion.

"I have a sense of humour too," Anwar said, tightening
his grip on Hunter's collar. "And this is how I express it!"

Hunter came back on even keel. He laughed again,
and said, "My friend, this is an artificial snake. Not the
real thing."

Anwar's grip on Hunter's collar loosened involuntarily.
"What?"

"Yes, artificial." Hunter smiled and touched the false
snake's head. "A rubber snake, with a mercury balance.
That's how its tongue flicks in and out."

"Wonderful!" Anwar smiled and let go of Hunter's
shirt. He reached out his hands, picked up the imitation
snake, and examined it closely. It was, to be sure, a work
of marvelous craftsmanship.

"Come, come. Let's go back." Hunter tried pulling

Anwar by the arm. "Let's go in. It'll be great entertainment."

Anwar walked along behind Hunter. The guests were on the move toward the adjoining hall.

"Where is everyone off to?" Hunter was surprised.

"Nowhere," Anwar informed him. "Dinner has been announced. They're moving into the adjoining hall to eat."

"But no one cut the cake?"

"In this house, they don't have that custom," Anwar said.

"Then when should I give her the present?"

"After the dinner."

"Isn't that a bit unusual?"

"This is one of those bastardized, half-European birthday celebrations," Anwar said, curling his lips in derision.

"Ha, ha!" Hunter Dunkitale guffawed again. "But you're part European yourself, a Eurasian, aren't you? Would you describe yourself as a bastard?"

"Most definitely; I am a Eurasian, and I stand by my words!"

The two arrived at the dinner hall. There were more than a couple of hundred guests at the table, and they had some difficulty in locating their seats among them. A couple of stewards were circulating with seating charts in hand. They assisted Anwar and Hunter in finding their places. The Dunkitales were at the same table as Anwar. The food had already been served, and everyone was busy eating. Anwar stared intently at the Dunkitales, but Hunter seemed to ignore him, as if he didn't know him at all.

The orchestra was playing lightly in the background, and hands were kept busy feeding mouths. The scene was bustling with activity, of people eating and serving food. The whole party seemed well-organized and pleasant.

Suddenly, the hall went dark. Many of the guests

exclaimed in surprise. Then a woman's piercing screams drowned out everything, orchestra and all. Anwar sprang up from his seat. He heard the sound of a table being overturned. The clatter of crockery being smashed rang through the dining area. The orchestra stopped. The din of confused noise and aimless shouting increased.

The lights came back on.

Shaheena was screaming, jumping, and leaping about again, as if she was doing a tribal war dance. She began to pull at her clothes, ripping them and throwing the shreds about frantically.

The guests stood for a moment, utterly bewildered and at a loss for what to do. Then pandemonium broke out. Everyone began shouting and cursing at the same time. Anwar saw Begum Irshad running madly toward Shaheena. "Oh, my little girl!" she was moaning. "Oh my Shaheena! Stop, my darling, stop!"

But Shaheena's frenzied hands would not be stopped. Within moments, she had no clothes left on her body but rags and ribbons. A number of women guests tried to restrain her, and finally, they managed to half-drag, half-carry her to another room.

The guests were perplexed, unsure what they should do under the circumstances. Should they leave without saying their goodbyes? Should they stay and help? No one seemed able to think or act coherently. Anwar, meanwhile, realized that someone must have seen through his disguise. What other explanation could there be for what had happened to Shaheena? He considered leaving, but it seemed difficult to go out without attracting attention. Also, his pigheadedness and tenacity worked against his leaving the scene of action.

But where were the Dunkitales? It suddenly occurred to him to see if they were in evidence. He looked intently around the hall, but he could only see young Hunter. Roger was nowhere to be found.

He was distracted by the loud voice of Begum Irshad, who was making an announcing through a portable microphone. "Ladies and gentleman," she said, barely controlling her sobs, "I'm so sorry. My daughter has had another strange fit. We are still trying to determine the cause of this sickness. I beg for your understanding at this time. I'm extremely sorry." She put away the microphone and broke down openly.

A number of guests tried to soothe her. Some went up to touch her or hold her hands.

"It's okay. Please. Don't be so distressed. She'll get well soon. It's okay."

A few ladies, perhaps relatives of Begum Irshad, escorted her out. Other guests began to move towards the door. Anwar felt that it was a good time for him to leave as well. He made his way to the main door, but Hunter Dunkitale saw him, and accosted him.

"What is all this, Mister? What am I going to do with my present now?"

"Guess you'll have to wait for the next birthday," Anwar answered glibly, and came away from the hall. But his thoughts were full of the Dunkitales.

There were a number of people going out through the main corridor, and a press of bodies had formed. As Anwar tried to gently elbow his way through, he felt a sharp prick in his left thigh. He stepped back, bewildered, and bumped into someone behind him.

"Watch where you're going, sir," the person said.

Anwar wanted to apologize and get out of the way, but he found that his body had become astonishingly light; he felt that if he raised his foot, he'd float off into the air. Hot flashes were surging through his body. The news story he'd read that morning, about Hameed being involved in a similar incident, flashed through his memory.

He managed to stumble and grope his way to the nearest wall. No one bothered to stop and ask what was wrong with him. He noticed the Dunkitales saunter off, but he was utterly immobile—there was no question of pursuit.

The corridor emptied in a few minutes. Anwar's thigh had started to hurt much worse. What started off as a little needle-prick now felt like a gunshot wound. It was difficult to remain standing, even with the wall supporting his back. He slid down until he was lying prone on the floor, helpless as an infant.

Anwar's breath came in gasps. He lay there like a pole-axed buffalo, scarcely able to bear the pain in his thigh, and restraining himself with some difficulty from groaning out loud. Despite all this, his faculties of reasoning were intact, and he realized that if a member of the household or one of the servants noticed him, he'd have to grin and bear the rants of Begum Irshad. It was possible that the lady was now bound for where he lay. Shaheena's predicament was because of his involvement. So one motive for paralyzing him might have been to provide Begum Irshad with an opportunity to give him such a bad tongue-lashing that he might never look towards Irshad Manzil, or Shaheena, ever again.

Anwar's reading wasn't wrong. Within minutes, Begum Irshad, followed by four servants, confronted him.

"Mister... Joseph... Peters," she said slowly, through gritted teeth, pronouncing each syllable with deliberation. Then she turned to the servants. "Pick him up," she commanded.

Anwar said nothing. He was, in fact, incapable of saying anything; his tongue was as immobile as the rest of his body. He could still think and see, but couldn't do much else.

The servants carried him roughly into a room where, at the orders of Begum Irshad, they dropped him into a big easy chair like a sack of coal. "Remove his clothes and turn the fans up to full speed," she said, and left.

The reclining chair on which Anwar lay had coffee tables surrounding it on three sides. On each there was a table fan going. Within moments, Anwar, now wearing only his underwear, could feel the chill blast from the three fans start working its way into his limbs. He recovered with astonishing speed. In just a quarter of an hour, he was his normal self again. The needle wound had subsided to a tiny prick.

"Please turn off the fans," Anwar told the servants. "And let me have my clothes. I am all right now."

His clothes were given back to him. One of the servants left the room, presumably to inform Begum Irshad about Anwar's state. He quickly put on his clothes, took a cigarette from his case, and was about to light up when he was summoned to go and see Begum Irshad in the drawing room.

Anwar followed a servant into the drawing room, still holding a burnt-out matchstick in his hand, the lit cigarette dangling from his lips. There was no invitation from Begum Irshad for him to sit. She shouted instantly as he entered, "What brought you to my house?"

Anwar dropped the matchstick on the carpet and replied insouciantly, "I was invited."

"You're lying! I'll have you hauled up before the courts. You're cheating my little girl. You are extracting money from her on false pretences."

"Well, dear Madam, your daughter owes me money. She borrowed ten thousand from me and lost it at the card table."

"Look, I'm going to warn you once more: You must stop

seeing her. If you don't, you'll come to a sorry end, and there will be no one to even shed a tear at your funeral."

"Oh, I know two prominent women of the city—a mother and daughter—who will most assuredly cry a few tears over my grave. But my dear Begum Sahiba, one thing surprises me; you knew how to cure this new ailment I was stricken with! Last night, Captain Hameed, an officer of the Criminal Investigation Department, was stricken with the exact same symptoms."

"Maybe I did, what of it?" she replied, with an insouciance to match Anwar's. "You cannot threaten or frighten me. I am well versed in the ways of the law."

"How is Shaheena now?"

"That's none of your business. You can leave now, quietly, with no further ado."

"And did Shaheena disclose to you my—that is, Joseph Peters'—real identity?"

"I know nothing. And I don't care either. But if you're not off my property within the next five minutes, I'll have you thrown out on the road."

Anwar picked up his hat from a table, finished his cigarette with a long drag, and lit another with the stub of the last one. Then he smiled, and said, "Begum Irshad, please do summon me if you find yourself in any kind of trouble."

He moved up to the door. Then, without turning, he said, "I'll keep my eyes on this building, though. Imagine that my spirit is hovering around."

He walked fast through the building and out of the compound. There was no suitable place where he could linger quietly, for there were bright lights everywhere. He would have thought of something, had there been fewer lights. He came out on the road.

It wasn't Anwar's usual style to walk away meekly in a situation like this. He was a man of an obdurate and avenging nature, one which he had never managed to soften. Last night at the Arlecchino, Begum Irshad had said harsh and insulting words to him. Now, here, she had done it again. And yet... was it possible that there was something else, or some*one* else, behind her actions? And if so, what—or who—could it be? Anwar stood on the pavement and pondered. At any rate, he needed to stop there and wait for a cruising taxi.

Why was Begum Irshad being forced to wander about in the narrow alleys and lanes of the city at night? Who was punishing her, and why was she permitting it? Why didn't she inform the police? Clearly, she wasn't afraid of them; if she had been, she would have had Anwar thrown out unceremoniously, rather than provide means for him to recover. She was aware that an officer of the Criminal Investigation Department had had the same experience, and that experience had also been publicized in the press. Then why did she take the extra trouble with Anwar? It had to be because her mysterious persecutor had instructed her to do so.

Should he stay here, and try to find that mystery man? But there was no reason to assume he would still be in the house. All things considered, it seemed pointless to stay; he had best get a move on. Besides, he should report to Colonel Faridi about what had transpired at the party. Hameed had had an almost identical experience, so perhaps Faridi could derive some points for thought or action from studying the event that had taken place at Irshad Manzil.

He also wondered a little more about Begum Irshad. Why had she made it so obvious that she knew the anti-dote to Anwar's symptoms of poisoning? Had she been forced to do so? Yet that didn't seem likely. For if the mystery man was behind Begum Irshad's action, then it followed that he wanted to attract the attention of the police. But then why should Anwar have become the object of his malice?

Anwar was so lost in thought, he didn't notice the motorcycle that came cruising to a stop just in front of him.

"So, were you thrown out?" he heard Rasheeda's voice ask derisively.

"Well, I would've been, if I'd stayed even a minute longer. Scoot over to the pillion, let me drive."

Rasheeda slipped back to the pillion. Anwar took the driving seat and sped away from the vicinity.

"Were you hoping for me to come by?" Rasheeda pinched Anwar in the back.

"Sit quietly, or I'll drive the bike up on the pavement."

"Go right ahead," said Rasheeda. "That would be a grand adventure indeed."

Anwar said nothing, but remained on the road.

"So today she had another fit, the same as yesterday," Rasheeda stated.

"How did you know?"

"Oh, I have my sources," Rasheeda boasted. "I also know the party came to an end because of it." Anwar held his tongue. He drove towards Faridi's residence. A few minutes later, they were there. The gate wasn't closed, so Anwar drove directly up to the portico. He was disappointed to find out that neither Faridi nor Hameed were home.

Rasheeda said, "Let's go home then. Why wait here?"

"No. I'd like to wait," Anwar said, crossing through the outer verandah into the living room and taking a seat. He was still in disguise; it was only because Rasheeda was with him that the servants allowed him to walk into the house so freely. They knew Rasheeda well.

"Have you reported the incident to the Colonel?" Rasheeda inquired.

Anwar asked, "Which incident?" Then he scowled at one of Faridi's servants who was standing in the doorway, staring intently at Anwar. The servant, unable to restrain his curiosity about the stranger, finally blurted out a question to Rasheeda: "Ma'am, where is Mr. Anwar?"

"Why, what's the matter?"

The servant said, "The Colonel wishes to speak to Mr. Anwar on the phone."

Rasheeda and Anwar looked at each other in surprise. Then Anwar, rising from his seat, said to the servant, "Okay, let's go. Where is the phone, then?"

The servant, still fooled by his disguised appearance and voice, gave Anwar a look of reproach for behaving like a joker.

"Come on! The Colonel must be waiting," Anwar said in his normal voice. The servant laughed with embarrassment. "Oh, so it's you, sir!" he said, and led Anwar to the phone.

Anwar picked up the receiver with some trepidation. Faridi spoke from the other end. "Go ahead, you can give me your report about having had an experience tonight just like the one Hameed had the night before. But what use will it be to me?"

"So you know already!" Anwar couldn't hide his astonishment.

"Just as well as the five fingers of a hand know each other," Faridi said matter-of-factly. "And I suppose you're also wondering why Begum Irshad gave you succour when she clearly bears malice against you?"

"You know about that, too? My God!"

"Yes. But I believe you are wasting your time."

"No, sir. I've already hit her up for ten thousand so far."

"I don't think Shaheena will have anything further to do with you. By the way, it saddens me to see how clumsy you are. They saw through your disguise with no trouble at all."

"I was sloppy, I confess."

"Right. But you must now quit acting in this matter."

"What if Shaheena forces me somehow?"

"My advice then would be for you to act openly."

"I don't follow you."

"You have nothing to fear from Begum Irshad. She can never take action against you."

"Look, sir... I presume that you also know why she's been wandering around the city late in the night, driving her buggy herself."

"No, I don't know anything about that yet. Nor do I want to know."

"Why is that, sir?"

"I'm more concerned with the criminal, rather than the crime. Anyway, you can go home now. Good night," Faridi said, and broke the connection.

7

Angel in Yellow

Hameed had his handkerchief wrapped tightly around his ears as protection from the cold. Yet his teeth were chattering, and the ice-cold steel of the GI pipe seemed to stick to his palms. He planted his feet on the windowsill as best he could and looked down. A fear even chillier than the weather gripped his heart. He was nearly sixty feet above the ground, and had another ten feet to climb before he would make it to the roof and get a chance to breathe easy.

Had he been inclined to let his bones be pulverized to dust, he would have let go of the pipe and beaten his forehead with his hands in despair. But he still had enough sense left to know that he had to keep holding onto it firmly with both hands. It was this pipe, after all, that had supported his climb all the way up to sixty feet, and would hopefully support him for the remaining ten, so that he might reach the roof of the building and get a new lease on life.

He was not alone on this hazardous mission. Father Hardstone was his travelling companion. But where was he now?

Hameed breathed a cold, deep sigh and continued to climb. He hadn't had any news from Father Hardstone for a while now. In reality it had only been three minutes, but Hameed felt like he'd been climbing up the wall for at least three thousand years. Colonel Faridi had reached the roof three minutes ago, and was apparently in too much of a hurry to look back and check on Hameed's state of body and mind.

Finally, Hameed managed to negotiate the remaining ten feet of wall and pipe. He was now on the flat roof of the five-storey building. He threw himself down on the hard surface, his chest heaving like an ironmonger's bellows. He was feeling so thoroughly disgusted with life that he felt like breaking out in song at the top of his voice:

Twinkle, twinkle, little star,
How I wonder what you are!

He lay there in a state of exhaustion for nearly ten minutes, until another problem occurred to him: How would he get down into the building? After a moment's deliberation, he realized that if getting down into the building had been at all perilous, then Faridi would have stayed back to guide him. With these thoughts in mind, he started to crawl on his stomach, making for the edge of the roof so as to get a better idea of the situation, and the possibilities of getting into the building. Why was he here? It was a question even his guardian angel couldn't have answered. In truth, Hameed had by now given up believing in the notion of a guardian angel keeping a protective eye over him. His angel apparently gave no attention to watching over him at all.

Reaching the edge of the roof, he peeped and smiled to himself in satisfaction. The floor immediately below the roof had an open terrace, well-lit and easy to reach, for the drop was less than fifteen feet. The lights meant that things were as they should be. Father Hardstone would never have left them on if the situation was dicey. Hameed groped with his foot for the skylight and slid carefully down to the sill of the skylight. It was now only twelve feet to the ground, and Hameed jumped comfortably, his heavy rubber shoes cushioning the fall.

Still, his jump must not have been entirely silent, for someone called out from a room on the other side of the terrace:

"Another angel! How lovely! How lucky I am!"

Bewildered, Hameed looked all around him. The voice emanated from a well-lit room whose doors and windows stood open invitingly. Then he saw Faridi, who was standing erect in the centre of the room, his hands comfortably in his pockets; a lit cigar was stuck between his teeth. Wisps of aromatic, grayish-blue smoke from the cigar floated up into the atmosphere of the room. Next to him, a very thin man with a lengthy beard was lying stretched out in a colonial-style easy chair with long side arms. He wore a yellow cloak that covered his entire body.

Hameed entered quietly, measuring every step. But the moment he entered the room, the thin yellow-cloaked man sprang up from the chair. His eyes lacked brightness and his cheeks were sunken. Still, he didn't look any older than thirty. He said in a solemn voice:

"I welcome you, O holy angel!" He stretched both his hands to Hameed. "I am truly fortunate."

Hameed extended his own hands to the thin man as well, with an equal show of solemnity; but the next moment the thin man flopped back into the long chair. Hameed noticed that even his face was a goldenish yellow. In fact, it was *he* who resembled some sort of angel.

"Sir, won't you tell me your name?" Faridi asked.

"My name is Loyal Dog," the man answered.

"I expect gravity and sobriety from a grave and sober person such as yourself," said Faridi.

He smiled. "I don't need to tell you my real name. We

angels can find out anything at all about anyone at all—I know it's not difficult for you."

"How long have you been here?"

"Since the beginning of creation."

"And where was I at that time?" Hameed muttered, looking around in bewilderment.

"Brother Marut, don't you remember? You were there too, hanging upside down by my side." He spoke in extremely grave tones.

"Oh? What did you say just now?" Hameed turned toward him and stared hard at him.

"Alack, my brother! Don't you remember that Greek Venus?"

"I've known plenty of Venuses, even some Japanese ones. You state your purpose."

"First, you must tell me where you have been all these millennia," the yellow-cloaked man said. "All that I remember is that there was an earthquake, and the Well of Babylon was shattered into a thousand shards. When I came to my senses, you were no longer there by my side... My God, Brother Marut, do you remember our thirst? Our tongues were hanging out, and there was the water only a palm's breadth away."

"Ah! Yes, yes, of course," Hameed nodded in agreement. "And we were hanging, er, upside down."

"Thank God you have remembered, dear brother. Where do you live now?"

"Oh, I live with Venus, in her house." Hameed winked at Faridi and smiled. But Faridi didn't seem the least bit interested in their babble.

"What!" The yellow-cloaked man sprang to his feet, and drew himself up to his full height. "You live with Venus?"

"That's right. And Mars is my brother-in-law."

"If such be the case, then you have reneged on your covenant. You have sinned, and I shall never forgive you."

Suddenly, Faridi raised his hand. "Are you, perhaps, called by the name of Harut?" he asked the yellow-cloaked man.

"Why don't you ask *him* what my name is?" The man gestured toward Hameed.

"Alright." Faridi looked at Hameed questioningly.

"Yes, it's true." Hameed nodded gravely. "This person is called Harut, and I am his brother Marut. As told in the legend, we were angels who fell in love with the Greek Venus, against the commandments of God. We were punished for our sins by being hung upside down in the Well of Babylon. Nowadays, I cobble old shoes, and as for him—he's a bookbinder, I think."

"Harut I have been since eternity without beginning, and Harut I shall remain until eternity without end. I consider it inelegant to act like a loafer one day and an angel the next."

"So you won't quarrel with me anymore about Venus, is that right?" said Hameed.

"Enough," Faridi muttered irascibly. Then he said to the yellow-cloaked one: "You will be reunited with your Venus, I promise you that. But you must not reveal to anyone the visit we angels have made here tonight."

"Yes. Remember well these instructions of my elder brother Izra'il," Hameed said, gesturing toward Faridi.

"Delighted, sir," the man said, bending low and shaking Faridi by the hand. "Why would I ever reveal it to anyone?"

Faridi took a chair, and gestured to Hameed to take one too.

"What would you prefer to drink, may I ask?" the yellow-cloaked man said deferentially.

"Oh, whatever happens to be available when needed,"

Faridi said airily, giving a wide yawn, in the manner of an alcoholic who has gone a long time without a drink.

"May I have the honour of pouring you two glasses of a Portuguese wine—a very fine, old vintage?"

"I'd be grateful," said Faridi. "But my rule is to pour my own drinks, and those of my companions as well."

"I would be pleased to honour the wishes of my guest." The yellow-cloaked man rose, unlocked a cabinet, and produced a bottle of port that was covered with cobwebs. Then he brought out a corkscrew and three glasses, and placed everything on a coffee table.

Hameed's eyes nearly bulged out of their sockets at the sight of the bottle of vintage port. He looked at Faridi in wonder, but said nothing. Faridi poured generous measures into three glasses. Then they all clinked glasses, and drank to each other's health. The very first sip hit Hameed like a blow; the sensation travelled from his throat to his brain, and then to his eyes. He felt his temples burning. The wine was excellent, but extremely strong and dry. The yellow-cloaked one drained his glass in three gulps and put it back down with a thump. Hameed did the same, but his throat, chest, and stomach were burning as never before. Then he, too, set his glass down with a thump of satisfaction and looked triumphantly at Faridi.

He was disconcerted to see that Faridi was glaring at him murderously. Then he also saw that Faridi's glass was untouched; he hadn't even taken a sip. Hameed was aghast. He had, quite thoughtlessly, assumed that the wine was for drinking.

"What have you done, you fool!" Faridi growled. Hameed tried to speak but his tongue and brain both failed him.

The yellow-cloaked man, reclining in his chair, was looking forlornly at the ceiling. "She will come. I am certain of it... She'll come," he muttered. He paused, then went on in the same tone:

"Centuries ago... Yes, centuries ago, I saw her bathing in a lake. Twilight caressed her face; a golden budgerow passed near her, held aloft by a giant swan... and the flowers of the elephants, they were floating, floating in the air..." He trailed off, and began to produce meaningless sounds, like an infant child. Soon, his neck slumped to one side; he became fully unconscious. Faridi tried to shake him awake, but without success.

The wine seemed to have been laced with something potent, and it was slowly seeping into Hameed's nervous system. His hands and legs felt numb, though his ability to think and feel wasn't yet impaired.

He watched Faridi putting the bottle and glasses back into the cabinet, then lift up the yellow-cloaked person and drop him in a double bed. Next, he came and grabbed Hameed by the collar, shook him violently, and said, "You fool, that wasn't just vintage wine. There was something else in it too. What will I do with you if you pass out and fall on your face?"

Hameed pointed toward the bed. "I'm an angel, too. Bury me with the other one."

"Wretch! How do you hope to get out of here? Will you be able to climb down the pipe?"

"No. Not a chance," Hameed said, making a futile attempt to clench his fists. "Impossible. I won't even be able to hold it."

"To hell with you," Faridi said, and went off to search the rest of the floor. Besides the terrace, there were three rooms, surrounded by a balcony. All of them were quite spacious, and the opulent appointments and furnishings revealed the yellow-cloaked man to be a person of substantial means. Hameed stumbled along close behind Faridi. Now his thinking, too, was becoming incoherent.

"Please introduce me to the father of that Greek Venus," he implored Faridi, touching him on the shoulder.

"Back. Get back," Faridi hissed, and pushed him away.

"Oh, so you think you can push me around, do you?" Hameed rolled up his sleeves. The wine had begun to seriously affect his brain.

"Don't tempt me."

"You'll see how I'll deal with you!" Hameed said, thumping his chest.

Faridi went back to his search. He was opening all the drawers, picking up and examining every article in sight.

"So? Have you lost your nerve?" Hameed jeered, swaying drunkenly.

But Faridi paid no heed. Then Hameed, too, began to pick things up and look at them, as Faridi was doing; unlike Faridi, though, Hameed would proceed to throw them about carelessly. Then he picked up a timepiece; after a cursory examination, he put his ear to it, and then began to say "tick, tock, tick, tock!" as if he was teasing the timepiece.

"This damn thing doesn't even know how to work properly," he said with irritation, and smashed the time-piece on the floor.

"What absurdity is this?" Faridi snarled.

"My dear elder brother, please attend to your business," Hameed put his hands out. "Stay there, don't make me lose my rag. Who do you think I am? Some ulloo ka pattha?"

"I'd skin you alive if you weren't so far gone."

"I'm not gone. Come, let's see you try and skin me alive. Let's see how powerful you really are."

Faridi scowled, and busied himself with trying to pick the number lock on a suitcase. Hameed's eye fell upon his reflection in a full-length mirror on the door of a wardrobe. He clenched his fist, gnashed his teeth, and stepped up to the cabinet, muttering:

"You bloody ulloo ka pattha, trying to disguise yourself as me! You idiot!"

He smashed his fist into the mirror, and then an expression of utter helplessness spread over his face; the mirror was so strong that it had withstood his blow. The effect on Hameed's hand and wrist bones, though, was another story.

Faridi turned to him and said coldly: "Have you gone completely out of your mind, you idiot? You'll compromise the whole operation."

"You're the idiot!" Hameed shouted. "I won't tolerate any more insults." Hameed opened the wardrobe and began to scatter its contents all over the room.

"What do you think you're doing now?" Faridi was really angry now.

"Enjoying myself," said Hameed.

"Right. Then enjoy this," Faridi said, advancing toward him. Hameed tried to lunge forward, but Faridi raised his right leg and gave him a kick. Hameed screamed and fell to the floor, his right shoulder hitting the ground with a thud. Writhing and bellowing like a wounded wild buffalo, he tried to rise, but Faridi had him at his mercy. Within a minute, Faridi had tied Hameed's ankles together with his own necktie, thus rendering him helpless.

Hameed, bent double, tried his best to untie the knots on his feet, but with no results. Fed up with everything, he held his hand over his ear like a street singer, and began to sing:

"Bulbulo, mat ro yahaan aansoo bahaana hai manaa
Inn qafas kay qaidiyon ko gul machaanaa hai manaa

Nightingales, please don't weep,
Weeping is forbidden here;

Captives in a cage, you aren't allowed
To make any sort of noise!"

"Quiet, or I'll gag you!" Faridi said, stamping his foot.

"Aaa! You won't even let me weep!" With his hand still on his ear, Hameed sang a line from another film song at the top of his lungs:

*"Tum mujhay ronay bhi naheen daetay /
Hai hai zaalim zamaana*

Alas, alas, you won't even let me weep!
Oh, the cruel, cruel world!"

Faridi began to slap him across the face, first on one side and then the other.

"Aaa! What's are you doing, my friend?" Hameed tried to stop Faridi, but it was impossible. Hameed's cheeks soon turned beetroot red.

"All right, go ahead... hit me! God will unleash his wrath upon you... how could you inflict so much pain on the heart of a poor old widow like me...!" Hameed blubbered and lay down on the floor, his face in his hands.

Faridi's eyes blazed with anger. Hameed presented a twofold problem. First, he was interrupting and disturbing Faridi's work. Second, he would soon become a security risk. They'd made a clandestine entry, since it was impossible to gain entrance to the building through the front door. The only way out was the same way they'd gotten in. The front door was securely locked from the outside. Faridi hadn't imagined that Hameed might actually drink the wine, or he would have given him a warning signal to him. The idea had been to put the man in the yellow cloak to sleep and do a thorough search of the building. That was why he had slipped a very strong pill into the wine bottle.

Anyway, he had to complete his job quickly. So he left Hameed as he was and addressed the work at hand. Faridi was that sort of person. He never worried himself over what might happen five minutes in the future.

He unlocked a trunk and began to go through it. Most of the contents appeared to be women's clothes and accessories; the other suitcases that he opened had contained women's things as well. He wondered why he hadn't been informed that there was a woman living there—if, in fact, one did. The information he had received was only this: that there was a mentally deranged man living in the building, with two men coming to attend to him by turns. Both attendants always locked the main door after they left. According to the reports Faridi had received, the mentally deranged man was always left very much alone at this time of the night. It wouldn't have been too hard for Faridi to pick the lock of the main door, but he hadn't wanted to leave tell-tale scratches on the door and lock. Now, though, thanks to Hameed's antics, it would be impossible to restore a look of normalcy to the place.

Hameed raised his head from his hands and screamed: "May your grave go up in smoke! May your whole body be devoured by worms!" He still seemed to be under the delusion that he was an inconsolable widow. "May you be denied the good fortune of reciting the Kalima before you die! Oh woe, woe is me, unlucky throughout my life... Ohhh, ohh, ohh... "

He wept and wailed, in the voice of a totally distraught and heartbroken woman.

A Counter-trick

Faridi laughed in spite of himself. He turned and said: "I'll call you to account for this when you're back in your right mind."

"Don't you tease me, or I'll start screaming!" Hameed seemed to have suddenly switched to playing the role of a younger woman.

Faridi was in a hurry to finish his search of the house. There was still a whole room to be gone through. He left Hameed to his own devices and entered the last room.

Hardly a minute had passed before he heard a strange noise. The panes of the window on his right began to shake; it sounded like someone was trying to open it.

Faridi tiptoed back through the doorway onto the terrace, closed the door, and stood behind it, with his eye pressed to the keyhole above the doorknob and his right hand on his revolver. He had the concentration and posture of a cat crouching in wait for its prey. He hadn't switched off the lights in the room, so he could see the moving panes of the window quite clearly through the keyhole.

Then the window panels were pushed open, and a man jumped into the room. He was dressed in tight black clothes and wore a black mask over his face. He stepped up softly to the very door behind which Faridi stood waiting.

Faridi watched the intruder attentively. The man was either a novice, or else quite daring, for he did not turn off the lights. Faridi noted that the intruder had taken the same route to enter the building as he and Hameed had taken, though while they had climbed all the way to the roof, the intruder had successfully crept along a ledge to reach the window.

Faridi stepped to the side of the door and stood motionless, with his back to the wall. He had turned off the terrace lights when he had begun his room-to-room search operation.

The intruder gently opened the door and walked onto the terrace. The very next moment, the barrel of Faridi's gun was at his neck. "Put your hands up," Faridi said.

The masked man raised his hands without protest. "Walk," Faridi said, prodding him.

They reached the door of the room where the yellow-cloaked man lay unconscious. "Open the door, quietly," Faridi ordered. The masked man pushed at the door with his foot and walked into the room, Faridi's gun still held to the back of his head. Faridi followed the masked man through the entrance—but he was in for a surprise.

The lights were on, but there was no sign of the yellow-cloaked man; in his place lay Captain Hameed, snoring softly on the bed.

Faridi had hardly had time to take in the new situation when he felt the cold barrels of not one but *three* guns pressing into his back and spine. He turned quickly, but his gun was snatched away even before he could complete the turn.

"Up with the hands," someone said. He spoke in English, with a foreign accent. Faridi raised his hands and heard someone laugh out aloud.

It was the masked intruder. He patted Faridi on the shoulder and jeered: "Hello, dear Mister Detective! Come on in. Don't worry, your assistant is out cold—there's no risk of our disturbing his beauty sleep."

Faridi stepped forward into the room.

"Sit," the masked man said, gesturing toward the easy chair.

Faridi smiled. "And if I decline?"

"Then your luck will have run out completely. Doctor Dread does not tolerate insubordination."

"I see. So *you* are the notorious Doctor Dread?"

"Are you surprised?"

"No. Why should I be surprised?" Faridi said, sounding unconcerned. "There's no shame in being bested by an opponent whose nose I've already rubbed twice in the dirt."*

"Ha, ha. I was simply entertaining myself both times, dear Colonel."

"And perhaps I'm entertaining myself this time," said Faridi, shrugging his shoulders.

"I know you are brave, and also clever," the masked man said coldly. "But I don't think you're familiar with my rules of operation. Whenever I come to a new country, I deliberately set up some dangerous situations for myself, just so as to acclimatize myself to the new environment. Do you follow? You must realize that if I had really wanted to bring about your demise, I could have done it with nothing more than a nod of my head. If Mary Singleton could

---

* Doctor Dread is a criminal mastermind with headquarters in San Antonio, New Mexico [sic], who is wanted by the American police for crimes including the murder of three U.S. senators. He is an expert in poisons. He first appeared in *Jasusi Dunya* #61, *Paani ka Dhuwaan* ("Smokewater"), and again in #62, *Laash kay Qahqahaa* ("The Laughing Corpse"). In both cases, Faridi managed to thwart his evil plans. – Ed.

prick Hameed's arm with a poisoned needle, couldn't she have just as well caused his instant death?"

"Yes, she could have," Faridi replied artlessly.

"Then what do you suppose could be the reason that the two of you still count yourselves among the living?"

"Because we have postponed the idea of dying for now!" Faridi said, smiling.

"But rest assured, this will be our last meeting."

"Most definitely, we'll come with you to the airport to bid you farewell."

"You misunderstand. I've decided I quite like this land of yours. The opportunities for making money here are excellent, much better than elsewhere. All that's left is to remove thorns like you from my path."

"And what do you plan to do about that other tiny little splinter, the one that's always causing you brain-aches?"

"You mean Finch?"* The masked man chortled. "He's nothing but my court jester."

"Nice, that's nice," Faridi said. "I'm amused."

"Now listen to me," the masked man said, his tone changing. "You're simply worthless next to me. You couldn't even understand the simplest of my moves. You kept chasing Mary Singleton, never giving a thought to why she went roaming around the city freely even after she pricked Captain Hameed with that needle... Didn't you even wonder how it happened that the crime reporter, Anwar, had a similar experience?"

"If Anwar *hadn't* had a similar experience, then I really would have wondered," Faridi said with a teasing smile.

---

* Finch is a diminutive man of Goan Portuguese descent who once worked as a circus performer in San Antonio. It was established in #62, *The Laughing Corpse*, that Finch and Doctor Dread have some sort of running feud, though Faridi and Hameed did not learn the cause of it. – Ed.

"Your men shadowing Mary Singleton tailed her to this building. Then you got the information from the neighbours that there was a madman living here, whose relatives kept him locked up inside," said the masked man, clearly relishing the opportunity to give a monologue. "Then we saw an interesting scene... Your assistant really is a complete fool! Look at what a problem he's created for you. Now you must be wondering what will happen to this fool—even if you somehow manage to escape."

"My dear Doctor Dread, you are indeed brilliant," Faridi said, putting as much awe and wonderment into his voice as possible. "Your words echo my exact thoughts. But listen, my friend. You're probably not aware that I've been secretly hoping to get rid of my assistant for a long time now."

"That's news to me!"

"Well, it's true. But hold on a moment. You know, it's really quite cowardly, the way you're treating me here. You have me disarmed, and yet there still are four guns pointing at me."

"In principle, what's wrong with that?"

"I don't care about your principles. It rankles to have all these guns on me. Ask one of your men to search me."

"Why?"

"So that you all can satisfy yourselves that I don't pose any threat. Then you can return your guns to their holsters."

"And why should I do as you say?"

"Well, it's only fair. According to what you just said yourself, my assistant and I only have a few minutes left to live. And the last request of a man about to die should always be fulfilled."

The masked man was silent for a few moments. Then he ordered his men to search Faridi.

The search was carried out thoroughly. Nothing was

found on Faridi's person that remotely resembled a weapon. The guns were put away. Faridi walked over and sat in the easy chair. "So, you were saying?" he prompted.

"Nothing, except... A few minutes ago, you were taunting me about Finch. Now I'm contemplating keeping you alive so you can watch me dispatch Finch with your own eyes."

"But Doctor... to tell the truth, I don't really care to live any longer."

"And why is that?"

"Oh, my heart's not in it. Who would want to live after such a crushing defeat as the one you've just dealt me?"

The masked man laughed, but Faridi's face still reflected misery and despair.

"No, I won't do it. I'll keep you as my prisoner until you've seen me squash Finch under my foot like the worm that he is."

Faridi pulled out a pocket watch that hung from a fob in his jacket. He shook it; then, putting it close to his ear, he said, "This wretched thing has stopped. Quite out of character for it. Perhaps it means this really *is* the last night of my life." He began to wind the watch. "What's the time now?" he asked.

The masked man looked at his own watch. "Half past two," he replied.

"Thanks," Faridi said, setting the watch. "But tell me, my dear friend Doctor Dread, who is this madman who lives in this house? I find him most intriguing."

The masked man burst out laughing. "I'll say this: he's the goose that lays the golden eggs. I can't reveal anything more at present. But remember, I can extract a gram of gold from every drop of a man's blood!"

"You certainly are a person of great powers and achievements," Faridi said admiringly. "But it's a fact that that little insect named Finch has made your life a living hell. You extract your gold by blackmailing others; but then he extracts his cut from you."

The masked man shrugged his shoulders, carelessly. "There will always be jackals that survive on the leftovers of the lions' kills."

"Yes, dear sir, that's a fact that can't be denied." Faridi's tone was again admiring. "Apart from men, you seem to be a great hunter of words as well!"

The masked man nodded. "Yes." Then he ordered his underlings, "Imprison these two!"

"You'll keep us prisoners *here*?" Faridi asked in surprise.

"Certainly," he said mockingly. "But it will be your mind that's imprisoned. Physically, you'll be entirely free. There will be no locks on the doors. You'll be free to go... but you'll always come back."

"I'm afraid I don't understand at all," Faridi said, looking completely baffled.

"A special injection will be administered to both of you. It will induce complete amnesia. You will remember nothing about your past life."

"Aha! How fascinating," Faridi said, and suddenly he stood up. In the same motion, he hurled his watch at the ceiling. Before any of the masked men could figure out what he was doing, there was a powerful explosion, and a blinding light that seemed to invade all their senses.

Hameed woke up screaming a piercing scream. The explosion appeared to have burned away his intoxication. The four masked men stood aghast, rigid and immobile. The room was heating up quickly. Within seconds, it was like a miniature hell. There were no flames, just an invisible cloud of heat, expanding and rising.

Faridi laughed softly. "Well, dear Doctor. Let's have a couple of bouts of arm-wrestling, shall we? Your tricks are famed all over the world. How will you counter this one?"

Driven practically insane by the heat, the masked men began to throw off their clothes one by one. Very soon, they were clothed only in their underwear. They'd clawed off their masks too, and now the masks lay on the floor, looking up at their owners in silent mockery. Surprisingly, Faridi and Hameed seemed unaffected by the heat.

Hameed left his bed and came to stand by Faridi's side. He looked at the four men with eyes opened wide in wonder.

"Tell me, Doctor Dread! How do you like my little rejoinder to the smoke-trick you used to escape at Rai Chandra Shekhar's?" Faridi said triumphantly.*

"What? This is Doctor Dread!?" Hameed exclaimed. He rubbed his eyes and stared at the half naked men.

"Yes, that's Dread right there," Faridi said, pointing to one of them.

"Ha! So let's tie them up and be done with him! What are we doing standing around?"

"No," Faridi said coldly. "Dread is very proud of his capabilities. He thought that he was giving us rope. He claims to find it entertaining to deliberately set up trouble for himself and then get away scot-free. He used Mary Singleton for no other purpose but to set a snare to trap us. So, Mr. Captain, there's no need to tie him up, for the time being at least."

"You really act in the strangest of ways."

Paying no attention to Hameed's words, Faridi turned to Doctor Dread and said, "Do you still have the physical strength left to attack us and do us harm?"

---

* A reference to Dread's escape at the end of #61, *Smokewater*. – Ed.

Dread remained silent.

"I know you don't. And that's why I won't arrest you now, in your present state."

"My dear Colonel! Sir!" Hameed waved both his hands in protest. "This isn't some detective novel, with you in the hero's role. Please, come back to your senses!"

Faridi shrugged his shoulders. "I am very much in my senses," he said. "Had *you* not been out of your senses, I could have captured Dread without needing to use that gizmo. But I owed him a magic trick, anyway."

"Perhaps I'm still drunk," Hameed muttered. He pinched himself on the arm, and gasped in pain. He was simply unable to believe his ears. He couldn't imagine that anyone in the whole wide world would let the notorious Doctor Dread get away once he'd been captured. What could Faridi be thinking?

"Please reconsider!" Hameed said, touching Faridi on the arm.

"Let's go." Faridi stepped resolutely forward toward the door, practically dragging Hameed along with him.

"I... But..." Hameed stared at Faridi, eyes dilated in wonder. Then he said softly, "Did you also... I mean, after me, did you maybe drink some of that wine yourself?"

"Come on, you idiot," Faridi said, pushing him.

They came outside. Faridi locked the door and told Hameed, "Rub your ears. Hard." Faridi began to rub his own ears, too. Hameed had no choice but to follow suit.

Hameed, helpless and shaken, was sniveling to himself. "If he himself is drunk, he doesn't think it's any sin. But if I commit even the tiniest mistake, he's ready to push me into the fires of hell."

"Are your ears warm yet?" asked Faridi.

"What the hell...!" Hameed had had enough. He dropped his hands. The very next moment, Faridi was rubbing Hameed's ears vigorously.

"Let go, for God's sake!"

"Are your ears warm enough?"

"Enough is enough! The bloody things have turned into kebabs! Let go now, please!"

"All right, come on," Faridi said, and started dragged him by the hand again. They came to the stairwell; they walked down fast and came to the front door, which now stood open. They walked toward Faridi's car, parked some distance away. Hameed's brain was now clear of the influence of the drink, but was clouded with anger at Faridi.

"What did you do back there?"

"Only what was necessary," Faridi answered nonchalantly.

"How could you let such a big fish slip from your net?!"

"Is your brain as stuffed full of hay as your mouth is?"

"I don't understand."

"That wasn't the real Doctor Dread. They are trying to unnerve and outwit me, and I am trying to unnerve and outwit them. I am human too, dear Captain; of course it's natural for every man, everywhere, to want to get one up on the other guy."

"And what would you say about an every-man who misses such an opportunity deliberately?"

"I'd call him a fool."

"Then what do you have to say about yourself?"

"Yes, I'm a big fool too. It was pure madness, wasn't it, for me to have let those fellows walk away after I played that trick on them? If you were to tell anyone else about what I did, they would think you were joking."

"Then tell me why, for God's sake! Were you drunk?"

"No. I never drink, my dear boy."

"Then please allow me to say that I have serious doubts about your sanity."

"You're quite welcome to keep doubting."

They got in the car. Faridi drove. "But what made them go stiff like that? And what was that explosion?" asked Hameed.

"Nothing really... just a trick that I've had up my sleeve for a while, expecting an encounter with Dread or some of his chief associates sooner or later."

"A trick? I don't follow."

"It had to do with your oil massages."

"I'm really at a loss. I can't tell if I'm speaking with Colonel Faridi or with that gigantic fool Qasim."

Faridi laughed briefly. "It was thanks to your massages that you could stand there safe and unharmed. Without them, you would have suffered the same fate as those hoodlums."

"What do you mean?" Hameed asked with astonishment.

"You seem to have developed an obsession with asking me what I mean."

"I've suffered from many other sorts of obsessions too. Now just one last obsession remains—that I should shoot you dead some day, and then shoot myself."

"No, I think you should shoot yourself first. Afterwards, if I consider it necessary, I'll ask you to shoot me as well. You stupid idiot, don't you realize why I've been having you massaged with that special oil every day?"

"Oh, those massages! I've been thinking that was because I recently went through labour."

"It was due to those massages that your limbs didn't become useless in that heat."

"My God! You've been planning this trick for that long?"

"Don't think too much about it. I keep a few tricks like that at the ready, at any given time. Don't forget that we're doing battle with no less a criminal than Doctor Dread."

"But how did that watch trick work?"

"It was a stun grenade, with the added capability of setting off a blinding flash and raising the ambient temperature dramatically within seconds. It works like a time bomb, in the sense that it has to be wound like a watch before it is set to explode."

"One of these days your laboratory is going to be our downfall."

"We won't be around to shed tears when that day comes."

"Pardon me, but this whole recent adventure is like the plot of some bad movie. *Shaku, Son of Bahram* or something," Hameed said, more out of pique than anything else.

"Sometimes truth is stranger than fiction."

After a few minutes' silence, Faridi said: "We should have given more thought to the matter of Mary Singleton. But yes, a reply to the good Doctor's tricks was also long overdue."

"I still don't think it was right for you to let those fellows go."

"Alright. But if I hadn't, who would have reported the story to Dread?"

"Wait, wait! Please, I want to know something. Who was it who used the needle on Anwar at Begum Irshad's party?"

"Who else but Begum Irshad herself?" Faridi answered. "And that was the one incident which should have prompted me to look into Mary Singleton's case more closely."

"Shouldn't you ask Begum Irshad to give a full and honest account of her actions?"

"That is, indeed, important. I'll certainly do it, and right away."

"Oh, I really can't understand anything that you do or say."

"That's lucky for me. Because the moment you begin to understand, you'll start claiming you're my equal."

"What is it that we don't know about Begum Irshad?"

"Do you know why the Doctor is blackmailing her?"

"No."

"I see," Faridi said sarcastically. "What you *do* know is that she has a child named Shaheena, who is young, good-looking, and unmarried. She smokes 555 brand cigarettes and claims to carry around 555 suitors in her handbag at all times."

"She's a strange girl. There's no doubt about it."

"You're an ass. Now let me think a bit."

"Please do," Hameed said nonchalantly, and slumped comfortably into his the seat.

"No, wait. First, explain to me why you drank that glass of wine, and so quickly at that."

"If you're the one offering, I'd be ready to drink kerosene, not to mention vintage port."

"You haven't yet developed a knack for understanding nuanced situations."

"Trying to understand nuanced situations always gives me an upset stomach."

"Enough. Now shut up."

Hameed went back to reclining in his seat and dozing. A few minutes later, their car stopped at the massive gate of Irshad Manzil. At exactly that moment, a horse-driven buggy arrived at the gate, and Faridi backed his car up to let the buggy go in. But the driver hurriedly turned the buggy around, and it headed back in the direction from which it came. There was no question of Faridi being slow to react on an occasion like this. In one smooth movement, he got out of the car and caught hold of the reins.

"Who is it?" came a woman's tremulous voice from the coachman's seat.

"Aha! Begum Irshad, in person," Faridi said pleasantly. "Nice to have met you here at the gate, or I would have had to go in and rouse your servants to inform you of my arrival."

"Who are you?"

"Colonel A. K. Faridi, of the Criminal Investigation Department."

"This late at night? Anyway, please state your purpose, sir."

"I didn't know I'd meet you in such circumstances."

"Please state your purpose. You shouldn't be concerned with my circumstances."

"One Mr. Joseph Peters has lodged a complaint against you."

"I don't know any Joseph Peters."

"He was among the invited guests at your daughter's birthday party. You became angry with him for some reason, and had him stripped, and made to sit in front of three electric fans. I'm sure you're aware that the continuous blast of three fans in this cold weather could well have given him pneumonia."

Begum Irshad looked stricken at Faridi's words. She said nothing.

9

Pursuit

"**M**a'am, I'm talking to you; please answer me."

"I don't know what to say." Her voice sounded tired, defeated. "It is true that I had him stripped by way of punishment. But will the law regard that as a crime?"

"In any country, the power to impose punishment vests only in the honourable courts. Citizens cannot be allowed to take the law into their own hands."

"He isn't really called Joseph Peters. His name is Anwar, and he is a crime reporter for *The New Star*."

"You don't say!" Faridi exclaimed in feigned surprise.

"Believe me. For no reason whatsoever, he is harassing my daughter. Wait, let me try and remember the name of that officer... Oh, I'm sorry, I've forgotten it. But just recently, at the Arlecchino, I gave Mr. Anwar a stern rebuke, and warned him, in the presence of an officer of your own department, to stay away from her... I can't recall the officer's name, though... And also, Anwar is trying to get my little daughter hooked on drugs! That very night, your officer found cocaine in his possession. Later, I believe, the matter was hushed up through the exchange of money. Anyway, that's not my concern. I warned Anwar not to have anything more to do with Shaheena, and yet he gate-crashed her birthday party in disguise. Now tell me, what would *you* do in such a situation?"

"I would hand him over to the police."

"Yes. I made a mistake in not doing so."

"My dear Begum Irshad, I have witnesses who say that they saw Joseph Peters' guest card on a dinner table in the party." Faridi's tone continued to convey surprise.

"It must have been Anwar who produced those witnesses," she said insouciantly.

"Naturally. The plaintiff always produces witnesses in support of his claim."

"Whatever it may be, those witnesses are lying.'"

"Well, you can challenge them in court—not here."

"In court!" Again, Begum Irshad's voice was trembling. There was silence for a few moments.

"Yes, ma'am, in court," Faridi said softly. "He intends to file a defamation suit against you. He alleges that you forced him to come to your daughter's party, even if in disguise."

"This is nothing but libel."

"That, too, you would need to prove in court."

"Then what is it that brings your gracious presence here?" she said, her voice dripping vitriol.

"I have presented myself before you because there is another, similar, case. You may have read in the papers that my assistant Captain Hameed recently had a strange experience in the Maypole. He felt a needle prick his arm, and within no time, he became immobile, his body entirely rigid."

"Yes, I think I did see some news item about that."

"A similar incident also occurred with Anwar in your house," Faridi said. "He too felt a needle prick him, in his thigh, and his body became rigid and immobile for some time."

"Oh my God! He's attacking from all angles!" she muttered.

"I'm sorry?"

"He's bent on doing me in, somehow or the other. And what else did he say?"

"He said that once his body became paralyzed, you had him moved to a room in your house. There, your servants stripped him down to his underwear and switched on three electric fans directly in front of him. Hit by the triple blasts of air, his lost powers began to return. Gradually he became quite all right."

"Really!" Begum Irshad breathed a deep breath. "Just see how that swine has twisted the story! He's trying his best to trap me in some legal proceedings. All that happened, my dear Colonel, was that I was furious and had his clothes removed; that's all that I did. I admit it. But I think anyone in my place would have acted the same way."

"So the second accusation is false?"

"Absolutely and entirely false, my dear sir. Just imagine... but I must admire his cleverness: with what care and elaboration he has hatched this plot against me! My God! I never could have dreamt up such a story as he has. That news item stated that your assistant's condition improved because of the effect of the breeze, so that wretch Anwar added the three fans to his story. I repeat, I did have him stripped, but the rest of his story is completely of his own invention! Oh, may God protect me from the likes of that man."

"So it's incorrect, his story?"

"False, utterly false."

"Thank you ma'am. Sorry to have troubled you." Saying this, Faridi let drop the reins from his hands and came back to his car and restarted it; then he switched his headlights on. The headlights hit the front of the carriage and Begum Irshad could be seen clearly in the coachman's seat, wrapped entirely in black.

"What was the point of that little waste of time?" asked Hameed as the car drove away.

"You just keep watching. I haven't wasted any time up to now."

"She's a wily one—slick as a whistle."

"Yes, Indeed."

"Yet today we saw her in such a sorry state. What does she do, after all, wandering all over?"

"The law can't impose any restriction on that."

"Shaheena seems very worried about her."

Faridi made no reply. The car ran on through deserted streets.

Suddenly Hameed wondered aloud: "Where are we going?"

"Back to where tonight's journey began. Those hoodlums should be getting their powers of movement back about now."

"So why did we leave them alone?"

"So we could do something else in the meantime."

Hameed sighed a deep sigh of helplessness, leaned his head back against the seat, and shut his eyes.

• • •

The four men were in a bad shape. If they tried to stand up, they would only last a few seconds before dropping down to the floor again, as if the life had left their bodies. Their tongues were hanging out, they were panting like exhausted pack animals.

After several minutes, one of them managed to crawl a few feet toward the door. He raised a trembling hand to the door handle, but couldn't push it down; his hand remained up in the air, shaking as if palsied. He seemed to have lost the coordination of his limbs. A number of times he touched the handle, but couldn't muster strength to open the door.

Half an hour passed. The heat generated by Faridi's bomb was now subsiding, and now the half-naked men were again feeling the effect of the cold weather. But they still didn't have the strength to rise and put on their clothes.

"Must... try... to... g-get up...," one of them said.

"N-no... Too... difficulll...," another tried to say, but his tongue was too twisted and frozen to finish the word.

Silence again reigned in the room. The man who had reached the door seemed to be the strongest of the four, for he was now trying to rise, supported by the door handle. He managed to stand, and stayed there shaking for some time, his body supported by the wall. Then he turned toward the rest, encouraging them to follow his lead. Supporting himself using the wall, like a child learning to walk, he crept toward his clothes that had been scattered around the room. Painstakingly, one by one, he put on his clothes. The others looked up at him pitifully, begging him for help.

"We're cold, too," one of them said in a feeble voice.

"Wait," the strong one said, "I'll clothe you all."

It took them twenty minutes to get dressed. The strong one still didn't have enough control over his limbs to do it any faster.

"I feel my strength coming back now that I'm dressed," he said to the others, trying to sound encouraging. He sat in a chair, watching his companions with worried eyes.

"I can't understand how those two managed to walk away unaffected!" one of them murmured.

No one answered. The strong one's body language clearly indicated that he didn't want to discuss the matter. His brow was crinkled and his eyes smouldered with malice. His upper lip was stretched tight like a bow and his lower lip curled in disgust. Eventually, he spoke.

"I don't approve of all this nonsense. In my opinion, when the enemy confronts us face to face, we should speak to him with tongues of fire."

"But what could we do?" one of them said slowly, for he was still unable to speak fluently. "We had to follow our orders. They outsmarted us. I couldn't ever have imagined that pocket watch could wreak such havoc."

The strong one raised his hand and said, "Okay, what's happened has happened. Let's not talk about it anymore. The question is: what should we do now?"

"It's simple. You don't suppose he left us here just because he was careless, do you?"

"I understand now. His men must be downstairs waiting for us."

"So what should we do?" another man inquired.

"Dump our guns somewhere. Then there won't be any evidence against us. We entered this country on valid passports, and our embassy will take care of us."

"Yes, but isn't there incriminating evidence in this place?"

"No, nothing."

"Then we are home free. We can just leave."

"No, let's think some more," one of them said. "This building was rented in my name, though I never came here in person. Mary Singleton has been coming here, though."

"Don't worry about that. Nobody will suspect Mary, she's too white-skinned."

"What's the harm in just staying here?" one of them asked.

The strong one, who was apparently the leader, said sharply, "Don't be stupid. We have to give a detailed report of what happened. Otherwise the Doctor will eat us all for breakfast."

After that, none of them dared to propose an alternative to leaving the building. Their minds were frantically busy trying to tackle the thorny problem of how to phrase their report to the Doctor. All of them were aware of the fate that usually befell the bearers of bad news.

After some thought, the leader spoke: "I have no doubt that the building is surrounded. Also, you must understand well that we didn't fool Faridi for a second: he knows that none of us is really the Doctor. The only reason he left is that he wants to shadow us and use us to get to him."

Once again, everyone fell silent.

When the silence became painful, one of them raised his hand and said: "Okay, I have an idea. I'll go to the Doctor and report. You three remain here."

"How do you propose to do that?" one of them asked.

"You'll see in a minute. Please follow me."

He took them to a room which faced the street. It had big, glazed windows whose glass was dusty and not fully transparent. "Don't put the lights on!" he hissed. Then he beckoned each of the three men to come closer. "Come near me, take my hand. Here, sit in this chair." He seated the three of them one by one in chairs arranged near the big window, and got another chair for himself.

"Somebody put the lights on," he said, "but be careful not to show yourself against the window."

When the lights came back on, they saw that instead of sitting in his chair, the one whose idea it had been to bring them to this room was lying quietly on the floor. On the fourth chair, a pillow and a globe-shaped flower vase were arranged to give the impression of a sitting man.

"What's that you've done? Are you out of your mind?" the leader asked.

"Nothing of the sort," said the man lying on the floor. He gestured towards the chairs and the window and said: "From outside, they'll see the silhouettes of four guys sitting quietly, engaged in polite conversation!"

"Well, it's an idea at least," said the leader.

"Now I'll crawl out and climb down the drainpipe on the other side," he said, and left.

• • •

"Hey, it's almost morning, sir! Are you dozing off??" Hameed said in a hoarse voice.

But the next moment Faridi's hand was pressing his arm. "I'll be damned," he said. "Do you see that...?"

He was pointing up to the fifth floor window, through which glazing four shadows could be descried dimly.

"Why, there they are, sitting comfortably," Hameed murmured.

"Yes, an early morning conference, it seems," Faridi mocked. "But look closely. Doesn't one of them appear to be a dummy? One shadow is entirely motionless, while the other three make a slight movement now and then."

Hameed tried to take a closer look, but Faridi was already out of the car. Pulling Hameed's arm, he said urgently, "That little trick of mine must have addled their brains. They're nervous—otherwise they wouldn't be acting so stupid. There's no phone in the building, so they can't report to Dread if they stay here."

They had arrived at the back of the building now. "Ah, good, I wasn't wrong," Faridi whispered, pressing Hameed's arm. "Look, look there."

A shadow crept out of a top floor window, climbed up to the roof, and crawled toward the gutter pipe.

Hameed said, "You could sit on the pavement and tell

fortunes, and you'd still be as wealthy and successful as you are now."

They watched the man slide down the pipe, reach the ground, and walk fast toward the street. Faridi and Hameed followed a short distance behind him, trying to look like a couple of tough night-birds, with their hats tilted over their foreheads, very nearly covering their eyes, and the collars of their greatcoats turned up to their ears.

"Ah, but he won't go on by foot. I remember now, I saw a car in the back alley. Hameed, go get the Lincoln. Hurry!"

Hameed ran fast toward Faridi's car. In the meantime, the criminals' car started and went off. Faridi was wringing his hands, not expecting Hameed to turn his car around and drive it back quickly enough. Within moments, though, he saw Hameed drive up, headlights blazing, and the passenger side door open. Faridi had to admit to himself that Hameed wasn't always entirely useless. The other car had barely turned the corner as the Lincoln slowed down in front of Faridi.

"Keep driving," Faridi said, jumping through the open door. "Go up ahead."

Hameed drove expertly, and soon they were on the tail of the fleeing car. Hameed muttered, "I don't know what I'm doing. I can't understand anything that's going on here."

"What is it that you don't understand?"

"The whole night has slipped away. I wonder if I'll be able to get any sleep at all."

"You can sleep to your heart's content today. I won't object."

"Are you sure that these fellows are part of the Doctor's mob? Couldn't it be Finch's gang, trying to create problems for the Doctor?"

"Finch? Not a chance. Finch always manages to evade the law. He's very clever—not a fool like Dread."

"You're calling Doctor Dread a fool!?"

"He's a fool alright; there's no doubt about that. I regard all criminals who try to assert their superiority over the forces of the law as stupid fools—it's their very boasting that becomes a hangman's noose for them. Criminals like Finch, on the other hand, generally sail away safe."

"But then why do they do it? Why do they try to assert their superiority over the forces of the law?"

"It's a kind of perverse obsession. It's in their nature, this desire to be seen as possessing some special powers. Just as an ordinary individual wants to make a name for himself in his chosen field of specialization, so some criminals want to blaze a new trail, to prove that they have abilities that set them apart from the others. Ordinary, run-of-the-mill criminals don't have the audacity to openly challenge the defenders of the law; but there are some who do. Dread is one such criminal, and it's his need to be seen as exceptional that will ultimately be his downfall."

"The reason for the feud between Doctor Dread and Finch hasn't ever come to light—or am I wrong?"

"No. We'll only learn the cause of it once one of them is captured."

The two cars sped on, one behind the other, through the most densely populated parts of the city. Finally the leading car turned into the neighborhood where the residences of foreign ambassadors were located. The driver stopped at the gate of a house; the gate was opened for him quickly, and he drove the car inside. Faridi did not tell Hameed to stop, so he drove the Lincoln on ahead.

"What are we are up to now?" Hameed murmured, when Faridi asked him to turn in the direction of home.

"We're not up to anything. We'll go back home now, and then to our beds."

"I'm about ready to let go of the wheel and jump out of the car!"

"Don't lose your head, my dear boy. Do you propose that we gatecrash into a foreign ambassador's residence? For that's where Dread is holed up. It'll be a tough job, capturing him."

Hameed made a sour face. "Sometimes you act like you've already bagged him; other times you start howling about capturing Finch. My youth is really being wasted away for nothing."

Faridi laughed softly and fell silent. His laughter must have meant something, but Hameed didn't understand what it was.

10

The Tiny Devil

The driver of the car they had been following went in through the driveway, stopped the car, and sprang out. He vaulted over the steps onto the front verandah, entirely unaware that he had been followed to the house. He was so nervous that he didn't even realize it when Faridi's car overtook his. And there was no question of him noticing the soundless motorcycle that stopped right next to his car as soon as Faridi had moved on.

He barged in, not bothering to ring the bell when he found the door open. He went through and found himself in a hallway. He walked through it quickly, reaching another door at the far end. It had a doorbell marked by a small red bulb that seemed to burn brightly in the dark corridor. The man rang it.

The door was opened at once. Someone came to the door and beckoned the newcomer inside. He walked through another door, went up a staircase, and arrived at a large room, which, aside from wall to wall carpeting, was completely bare. He stood expectant, apprehensive.

A few minutes later, a door on his left opened and a tall man entered. His face was pinched, his thin lips pursed into a menacing line. The most arresting feature of his face was his sharp, bright eyes.

"Why the red signal?" he asked quietly.

Panting nervously, the visitor narrated the whole story, then said, "Doctor, sir, if I hadn't used these tactics, it would have been impossible for me to reach here."

"Tactics!" A bitter smile appeared on the Doctor's face. He scowled at him and said, "Couldn't you have given me your report from a phone booth? What was the need to come running blindly to this place?"

"I thought... I thought..." He tried to say something, but he could not articulate any defence.

"Talk whatever gibberish you want. Has Faridi ever before been stupid enough to be deceived by the 'tactics' of idiots like you?"

The man remained silent.

The Doctor went on: "What was the harm in all of you staying put till morning?"

"I... I thought..."

"You thought nothing! You have no ability to think. Don't you realize that if he'd wanted to arrest you, he could have done it for the simple reason that you were in possession of unlicensed weapons?"

"I am sorry if I made a mistake, sir."

"Don't talk rubbish. If you were truly ashamed of your mistakes, then you wouldn't keep making them.'"

The man stood silent, his head bent.

The Doctor said: "He left you alone so that he would be able to reach me through you."

"Oh God! What have I done?" The man struck his forehead in remorse and fear.

"I have no doubt that Faridi followed you here."

"So what will happen now?"

"I suppose if I asked *you* for advice, you'd tell me to get out of here, running blindly away just like you did."

The man made no reply.

The Doctor went on: "You fellows had better start

showing some sense, or I'll have to knock it into your heads."

"Please forgive me this last time," the man pleaded. "Actually, the effects of that infernal heat are still upon me."

The Doctor made a face. "I don't know why I have become so merciful..."

Before he could finish, one of the windows opened with a loud rattle and a tiny man glided in, gun in hand. His face was black, his lips painted a hideous red, and he was clad in tight black clothes from head to foot. The words "Devil ½" were inscribed on his chest in white letters.

"Truly," the man said in a sing-song voice, "it is a shame that you've become so tender-hearted. But you had better not try to get tough now with me! It's been a long time since I saw you so close. Put your hands up."

The Doctor's hands went up. His man followed suit.

"These men of yours are really quite idiotic. Whether or not Faridi has discovered your hideout today, I have."

"Go, don't waste my time," the Doctor said, in a voice that a grown up might use with a child. He also dropped his hands.

"Doctor Dread, this is the last night of your life. Put your hands back up!" the tiny devil said.

The Doctor raised his hands again. The tiny devil went on: "Today, I, a simple circus clown, will butcher you—and the entire world will be struck with wonder."

"Shut up!" the Doctor roared, and stamped his foot. A strange sort of light began to spread around the skylight, but the glow remained confined to the ceiling. No one paid any attention to it.

The tiny devil said, "Dear Doctor, you stand over me like a star—so far above me that when you roar, the sound will take another one thousand two hundred and seventy-five years to reach me. But the screams of that orphan girl are ringing in my ears *now*, and always. She was just thirteen, Doctor, a little girl of thirteen, when you ruthlessly made her the victim of your lust. The next morning her body lay there on the pavement, mocking the tall multi-storey buildings."

The Doctor dropped his hands again. As if he had no other care in the world, he addressed his minion: "I had a late night last night. Now you've come and disturbed my sleep. I'm terribly angry."

"Have no fear, Doctor. That'll soon be taken care of," the tiny devil said pleasantly. "I'll put you so soundly to sleep that these fools will never be able to wake you up again. People all over the world have wondered at tales of your dastardly deeds, so let your death be a cause of wonderment as well. How extremely wondrous it will be! The great Doctor Dread, killed by a little midget from the circus! Ha, Ha! A harmless little circus clown!"

He paused, then spoke through gritted teeth, "I was a good man, once. I earned my living by honest labour. But the screams of that poor little girl set me on a collision course with you, Doctor Dread. Now I know there's nothing I can't accomplish, nothing that's beyond my power! Why should I stay there in the circus, with my hands on my belly like a beggar? Why should I spend my life entertaining men who hoard ill-gotten wealth, when I can so easily lay my hands on their riches myself? Doctor Dread, prepare to meet your maker!"

Suddenly, the tiny devil's pistol spat flame. At the same time, his whole body trembled all over. The light from the ceiling was now flashing and coruscating everywhere like blue lightning. The tiny devil was dazzled, almost blinded. Naturally, his aim went wild. He leapt and fired, leapt and fired; with each shot, the blinding, nerve-shattering blue lightning flashed, sending the bullet awry. The Doctor laughed aloud at the sound of each gunshot, mocking the tiny devil.

Finally, the firing pin of the tiny devil's gun went down and produced only a click instead of a bullet; all the rounds had been used. The Doctor shouted to his minion: "Catch him now! Catch that foul brute!"

The Doctor's minion, who had been standing awestruck watching the proceedings, now came to life. He lunged forward at the tiny devil, but failed to lay his hands on him—for the tiny devil brought his feet together and gave him a sledgehammer kick to the face. The man uttered a cry of pain and fell backwards, landing on the floor with a thud. Next it was the Doctor's turn to lunge, but the tiny devil quickly moved aside, and the Doctor, losing his balance, fell on his face. Now the tiny devil had a knife in his hand, which he flicked open. The Doctor called upon his minion again to come back into action. This time, the man didn't make the mistake of rushing at the tiny devil. He crept forward, alert and slightly hunched, circling him like a street fighter, his eyes never leaving the knife. The tiny devil's eyes were unmoving, like those of a snake getting ready to strike.

Before the Doctor's minion could come within striking distance, the tiny devil vaulted at him. A long scream of pain and rage reverberated through the room. Just then, someone began rattling and pounding at the door. The tiny devil sprang towards the window, which was still open—but the Doctor was quick too, and he jumped at the tiny devil with surprising speed. The tiny devil turned, knife in hand, but this time the point of the knife only scraped against the wall. Dread had escaped by the skin of his teeth. The rattling and knocking at the door continued.

By the time the Doctor recovered his balance, the tiny devil had disappeared. Heedless of the racket at the door, Dread leaned over the windowsill and opened his eyes wide, trying to penetrate the darkness outside. He stood like this for almost a couple of minutes. The rattling and pounding continued unabated, but the Doctor appeared completely unconcerned.

Finally, he turned and cast a sidelong glance at the man on the ground, whose blood was still bubbling forth from some major vein in his chest. The blood was partially absorbed by the carpet, leaving a dark stain. Without making any effort to find out whether the man was dead or alive, the Doctor walked over to the door, which was still being rattled.

He opened the door, and the man in the yellow cloak barged in, almost knocking him over.

The Doctor shook the man like a dog, and pushed him away. "So it's you! Why were you knocking away at the door?"

The yellow-cloaked person stood silent for a moment, blinking his eyes. Then he said: "I am an angel. Don't raise your voice with me. I'm looking for my angelic companion, who was with me some time ago. Can you help me find him?"

"Go away, go to bed," the Doctor said, waving him off. "You're always waking up suddenly and spouting drivel. You must have had a dream."

"You're the one who's spouting drivel. The Angel of Death was there with my friend as well. The three of us drank at the same table."

"Will you go away, or should I get my hunting whip?"

"I'll go," the yellow-cloaked angel said, waving his hands. "But I will put a curse on you. Your boat will surely sink. Noah's deluge will come again. Then each and every one of you shall drown!"

Dread pushed him through the doorway. "Get lost," he said, and shut the door.

• • •

The clock struck ten. Captain Hameed rolled over onto his other side and made a face of displeasure, as if someone was trying to awaken him against his wishes. He and Faridi had reached home at about five in the morning. Hameed had jumped under the sheets fully clothed and with his shoes still on his feet, and had fallen asleep at once. Now the chiming of the clock had woken him, and he couldn't get back to sleep.

Finally, he rose. Showing a closed fist to the tick-tocking clock, he growled, "A curse upon your inventor!" Then he made a contented face, as if the clock had been deeply affected by his imprecation. On his way to the bathroom, he encountered Faridi, who was in the inner verandah, reading the paper. But this wasn't a normal time to be reading the paper; and in any case, Faridi's presence there was unusual. Faridi invariably left for work at a quarter to ten.

"Hello! How come you woke up?" Faridi asked, putting aside the paper.

"A dream got stuck halfway through," he said airily, and went into the bathroom.

When Hameed came out of the bathroom some time later, Faridi was no longer there; he learned from the servants that he had left. Hameed prepared for the day slowly, like a lazy person, or one who goes about doing everything sedately. At eleven o'clock sharp, a phone call came from Faridi, summoning him to the neighborhood where the ambassadors' residences were.

Irritated and in a foul mood, Hameed put on his wide-bottomed pajamas. Having done so, his eye fell on his reflection in the full-length mirror, and he became even more irritated. Fuming, he shuffled through the contents of a suitcase and took out a sherwani. A poet friend of his had left it there in exchange for a suit—a suit that Hameed had enthusiastically had tailored for himself, but had never had a chance to put on.

The story of the suit was that his friend, who fancied himself a "poet of the people", had found a fan in a rich girl who had invited him to tea. Of course, such an opportunity was enough for the poet to have all pretensions of being "of the people" blown clear out of his head. So he had come to Hameed's house, left his own clothes there, changed into Hameed's best suit, and then disappeared so effectively that it was only now, five years later, that Hameed even recalled that he still had his sherwani.

Hameed put on the sherwani, looked in the mirror again, and became even angrier. The contents of his suitcase were by now scattered every which way, and an old Turkish fez, tassel and all, was prominently visible. Hameed picked it up and put it on his head, though it was a tight fit. He took one last look in the mirror, and immediately felt the urge to smash it to pieces—but he restrained himself, and came out of his room.

The servants who saw him averted their faces and tried not to smile. Hameed noticed this, and burst out at them like a smouldering volcano. "What the hell are you laughing at, you stuffy oafs?"

Fortunately, no one answered; all the servants quickly found something they had to do far away from Hameed's presence. Hameed then wheeled out his motorcycle and rode off to the place where Faridi had summoned him. The wide bottoms of his pajamas were fluttering away merrily, and the tassel of his fez flew behind his head like a pennant.

He found Faridi on the grounds of the residence to which they had followed Dread's man the night before. Faridi wasn't by himself; he was accompanied by a number of men in uniform. Hameed felt horribly embarrassed. He had assumed that Faridi would be alone—but even the Inspector General of Police was present here. Everybody looked at Hameed's strange costume in astonishment. Those who knew him averted their eyes and smiled.

Faridi expressed neither surprise nor displeasure. Instead, he spoke with Hameed in his usual tone, apparently finding nothing inappropriate about Hameed's clothing. He was telling Hameed something about a body, but Hameed's mind was elsewhere. He was worried that Faridi would call him to account sooner or later.

Instead of chastising him, though, Faridi took Hameed by the hand and led him into the building. He said to him softly, "The body belongs to one of the four men from last night."

"Then Dread must have finished him off?"

"Maybe, but I have my doubts. I'm certain that he wasn't killed in the same place where his body was found."

They entered a corridor. The body was still lying there. "How do you conclude that he wasn't killed here?"

"His clothes are matted with dried blood, but there is only a light bloodstain on the floor. It doesn't look like that much blood has flowed here."

"And what do they know about the victim?"

"He was a relative of an embassy staffer, only recently arrived in the country."

"You must have seen his passport."

"Yes, and there's nothing fake about it."

"How could it be fake when he was connected with the embassy?"

"That's not a valid deduction."

"Do you think Doctor Dread is still here?"

"Did I ever say I expected to find Dread here? I don't remember expressing such a view."

"Then what did this guy come here for? Was it just idle curiosity?"

"How can we be sure this is the same man we followed last night? We didn't see that one's face. We recognize him as one of the four we met in that building, but that's all we can be sure of."

"So what is your conclusion?"

"I don't have any, for the present. Why are you always so impatient for conclusions?"

"So that the case can be wrapped up quickly, and I may be set free."

"There's no possibility of a quick conclusion here."

Hameed could do nothing but sigh. After a few moments, he asked: "Why did you summon me here?"

"Just to show you this. Had I attempted to enter this building last night, this body would have been quietly disposed of. These people wouldn't have been so bold as to dump the body here and report it to the police."

"What did we gain by not entering?"

"These people are under the spotlight now. Otherwise, the embassy could have claimed that it had nothing to do with the private lives of its employees or their relatives. And I might even have been persuaded that it was true. But now..."

Faridi stopped in mid-sentence. Then he said, "Come with me."

They came out of the building into the compound.

Hameed whispered to Faridi: "Shouldn't we search the building?"

"I already did, and found neither Dread nor anyone who could be a part of his gang. One of the walls in a room upstairs does, however, bear certain marks."

"I don't understand."

"Marks that were clearly made by bullets."

"Good! Then..."

"Then nothing, Hameed Saheb. Bullet holes do not incriminate a person residing in a building. A man is perfectly entitled to own firearms, and if he does own them, no law in the world can prevent him from using them to turn his wall into a sieve if he so pleases."

"Then why are we wasting our time here?"

Faridi gave no reply to this. He was lost in thought. Hameed looked around, feeling redundant. He wanted to leave as soon as possible, for very nearly all the police officers were scowling at him.

"Do I have your permission to go now? I was just about to leave for a poetry reading when your phone call came. I was deprived of the privilege of presiding over the musha'ira."

"Shut your bloody trap," Faridi said harshly. Abruptly, he stormed off toward his car. Hameed followed him, walking at a fast clip, but before he could catch up with him, Faridi had gotten into his Lincoln and started it. There was no point in Hameed trying to run and chase the car; he had his motorcycle with him anyway.

The car sped ahead. Hameed rode his motorcycle furiously, trying to keep pace. His insides were churning with resentment as they raced through the busy streets. He couldn't understand why he was being made to chase after the Lincoln like this. Why had Faridi dashed off so suddenly, and where was he headed? Couldn't he at least give him a chance to pull up alongside and ask where the next stop would be? Besides, he still wasn't satisfied with Faridi's explanation of his strange behavior the night before.

Nevertheless, his motorcycle sped on behind Faridi's car.

The Girl Again

Hameed finally managed to bring his motorcycle up alongside Faridi's car. But Faridi shouted loudly, "Get away from me!"

"Then why did you summon me?"

"Well it wasn't so you could report for duty looking ready to one-up a clown! Rest assured, you'll pay for these little antics. You have breached the limits of discipline while on the job."

Hameed turned his bike away from Faridi's car at the next turn. Qasim's favourite phrase, which he used to express contempt or frustration, was echoing in his mind: "My pf-foot, I don't care!" Hameed resolved to go to office wearing the same clothes he was wearing now, discipline be damned. Let the Colonel take exception to his clothing! Let him say it was a breach of discipline! *My pf-foot, I don't care!*

Like a typical political leader with a frog-in-the-well mentality, Hameed now started to think in platitudes on the subject of wearing the National Dress. In his mind, he composed an elaborate speech defending the merits of wearing pajamas and sherwanis and fezzes, even as his motorcycle went roaring through the streets and avenues.

Finally, he arrived at the office. Everyone who laid eyes on his new costume doubled up with laughter. But nothing shook Hameed's serious, determined expression. He sat in his office and made himself comfortable, idly rifling through papers, opening and shutting the files of cases both old and current, and didn't get up again until it was closing time. Inspector Rekha passed him several times during the day, but refrained from commenting on his clothing. Hameed went on acting as if he dressed that way every day, though the fact of the matter was that no one at the office had ever seen him wearing a pajama before.

In the evening, when he was on his way to the shed to get his motorbike, he encountered Rekha again. This time, Rekha smiled and said, "What's the story behind this new fashion of yours, Hameed?"

"Why?" Hameed barked, sounding as if he was about to tear her to pieces.

"Because a mullah has lodged a report about a stolen box of clothes."

Hameed was genuinely annoyed. "You can't make fun of my national dress!"

"Oh, and which nation do you belong to?" Rekha asked, her voice full of sarcasm. "I wasn't aware that you, too, belong to that band of jokers who talk so sanctimoniously about upholding national traditions."

"Hold your tongue, or you'll regret it."

"You know, you look a little like a hoopoe in this national dress of yours."

Nettled, Hameed kick-started his motorbike. Rekha cried, "Oh, Son of the Nation—I just remembered. There's a message for you from a foreign girl. Her name is Mary Singleton."

Hameed shut off the engine promptly. "What?" he asked in astonishment. Only he and Faridi knew about Mary Singleton.

"She says she'll meet you tonight at nine at the Maypole. There was a phone call while you were out. I forgot to tell you."

"Thanks," Hameed murmured, lost in thought. Then he restarted his bike. "Okay, I'm off now, goodbye."

He went home. Faridi was already there. Hameed got rid of his "national dress" and made his way to the bathroom. His nationalistic sentiment had begun as a joke, but at the office, the joke had escalated, and he'd developed a sort of brain fever. The more people had smiled at him, the higher his temperature had risen. The mere mention of Mary Singleton, however, had been enough to bring the fever down to normal. Now he set aside not only his "national dress", but also the fiery, passionate, patriotic speeches that he'd been mentally composing all day. Now, instead, he thought: *All the world's people are brothers and sisters; some are made from black clay, others from white. So what? The earth is one, and the sky that shelters it is one as well.*

As he went on thinking this way, he soon managed to forget everything he had learned about the beautiful Mary Singleton. What Doctor Dread's own thugs had said about the girl was now a distant memory. It didn't even matter that he himself had suffered bitter and painful treatment at her hands. There was no good explanation for this, except that perhaps Hameed's stars had wandered off course, and were now travelling in retrograde motion.

Hameed arrived at the Maypole at eight o'clock sharp. It wasn't as though Mary Singleton was supposed to be there yet; according to Rekha, Mary had said she would meet him at nine.

It would be wrong to say that Hameed had been careless in agreeing to the meeting. He had actually given quite a bit of thought to the matter, from many different angles.

But he had long ago gotten it into his head that Mary was innocent, and even now he found himself unable to consider her otherwise. He was, of course, ready to concede that she might be working with Doctor Dread, but he was sure that she was ignorant of her boss's true identity. Hameed could think of hundreds of examples of cases where people had been similarly deceived. So he clung to his notions.

At nine o'clock sharp, he saw Mary Singleton come in. He beckoned to her, and she pressed toward him eagerly through the crowd. Watching the way she walked, Hameed thought he would die a thousand deaths. He kept his eyes glued to her the whole way. Her every action was brimming with sex appeal.

Mary Singleton had smiled when she first spotted him, but by the time she reached him, she seemed somewhat flustered. Hameed welcomed her with a very warm smile.

She said in a trembling voice, "Actually, I came here to confess my crime."

"Oh, don't worry about it," Hameed said airily.

"Sir, I'm surprised at your attitude!"

"Why?"

"You're looking at a criminal."

"I think you've been caught in a trap. You've been used."

"How could you know that?" she asked in surprise.

"I just know."

"I had just about decided that it would be impossible for me to get *out* of the trap."

"No reason to let that thought get into your head. I knew the truth about you on that very day."

"What very day?"

"That day you pricked my arm with the needle. You were scared then, badly scared."

"And then when I saw your name in the paper, I almost died of fright. I knew at once that I had been duped."

"How did it happen? Let's have some details."

"You see, I come from a strict Roman Catholic family. I was brought up to be God-fearing and devout. I don't like the Protestants, I mean I really despise them. A little while ago, I happened to make the acquaintance of a Roman Catholic priest. We began to meet now and then. One day, he told me that a group of Protestants were planning to cause injury to our people, and asked if I would be willing to join hands with a group of like-minded individuals to defend our sect. I agreed immediately. The night that I met you, I had come here to see a man from our group. He told me in a frightened voice that he had seen some men here from the enemy group, and that they might be sitting in wait for us. He said things were likely to get ugly. Then he gave me a needle, and told me that if anything happened, if anyone seemed to be threatening me, I should stick them with it.

"Then you came to my table. I believed that you were the one I had been warned about. So, I pricked you with the needle and made off. That's all. That's my story."

"But then afterwards, how did you begin to suspect them? Did they point me out, specifically, as the enemy?"

"No. They didn't."

"Then what aroused your suspicion?"

"I'm too ashamed to tell you. Isn't it enough to say that there's a gang of criminals out there ensnaring innocent, inexperienced girls?"

"You have to tell me about it. You know which department I work in."

"Well... see, there is a building on Tariq Road... it's called the Tanvir Building. There's an angel-faced man living there, on the third floor. According to the priest, he was once a man of great erudition, a pillar of the Roman Catholic faith. But an adversary sect had ruined his life. They fed him some potent drug which destroyed his sense of reason, and now he leads the life of a confined mental patient. They told me I could earn merit in the eyes of God by taking care of him.

"I agreed... Oh, but I don't know if I can go on. I feel tongue-tied from shame."

"No, no, you must tell me."

"One day, he tried to molest me. I resisted him with all my strength. He laughed and said that lots of girls used to be brought to him, under the pretext of caring for him. Somehow, I saved myself from that beast. Now, after two days of cogitation, I sit here before you."

"You needn't worry any longer. I'll take care of this gang for you. Do you know where they operate from?"

"Yes."

"Tell me. I'll root them out and destroy them."

"They live in a dirty slum in Arjun Pura."

"Arjun Pura?" Hameed echoed in surprise.

"Yes. They claim to preach and minister to the poor of that area."

"Do you have the address?"

"I couldn't describe it. It's down a series of small, twisting, forking lanes. But I could take you there, to the house where they live."

"Sure. I'm ready to go right now."

"Good, and I'm ready to come with you. My heart is full of righteous anger at them."

Suddenly, Hameed looked up and saw that Qasim was there, and heading towards them. He was so surprised he couldn't speak. Before he could ask Mary to get up and follow him out, Qasim loomed over them.

"G-g-good evening, brother Ghameed!" Qasim said,

pulling up a chair and seating himself down in it. Mary looked a little nervous. Hameed was in the same state himself.

"Hee hee hee, dear brother Ghameed, I have pf-found you! I've b-b-been searching all over for you, but not a trace of you anywhere!"

"I'm not in the best of moods at the moment," Hameed said softly, in Urdu.

"Doesn't understand Urdu, does she?"

"Go away from here. Now."

"Her older shickster didn't show up?"

"Qasim, no more jabbering. Go quietly."

"I *won't* go! Hee hee! Let's see what you do about it! Hee hee!" It was surprising that Qasim was being so loquacious; normally, in the presence of women, he would be too flustered to even move his limbs.

"I'll hand you over to the police," Hameed threatened him.

"You can hand me over to mad dogs if you want. But I must meet her older shickster. Do introduce me. Pf-please!"

"You've got it wrong. This isn't the same girl from that evening," Hameed said, changing his manner.

"Go try to pf-fool someone else—you don't fool me at all. Hee hee!"

"Dear Qasim, please believe me."

"Why should I? Am I b-b-blind?"

Truly annoyed now, Hameed turned to Mary. "Come, let's go," he said.

"Who is this gentleman? What's he saying?"

"Oh, he's just one of *those*. Come on."

Hearing this, Qasim lost his temper. "What!? Maybe *you're* a one-of-those, b-b-but not me! It's *you*! You're the ton of hose!"

"What's the matter, sir? Why are you upset?" Mary asked, addressing Qasim.

"It's not a question of pf-feeling upf-set. This man is a cheat!" Qasim said with a scowl. "You musn't go anywhere with him. He'll pf-push you down a dell somewhere. I mean down a well."

Mary burst out laughing at Qasim's strange way of speaking. Qasim was overjoyed to have provoked this reaction; Hameed, meanwhile, was becoming desperately anxious. "Come on," he said to Mary. "Get up. Look sharp."

"No! This friend of yours seems like a very interesting person!"

Qasim's grin was widening with every moment, and now seemed to reach from one ear to the other. "No!" he said to Hameed. "She won't go with you at all. And if you try to pf-force the issue, there'll be murder here! To hell with you, you go on your way! Who do you think you are?"

"Qasim, I'm going to settle scores with you later," Hameed said in Urdu. He was really surprised at the transformation that seemed to have come over Qasim.

"My pf-foot! Am I weaker than you? Do you think you're the only one who knows how to enjoy himself?"

Mary produced a bar of chocolate from her bag. Qasim's eyes fell upon it at once, and he began to work his jaw up and down hungrily. Now Hameed was feeling upset with Mary too. Why wouldn't the girl get up? He looked over at Qasim, who was staring transfixed at the chocolate with a greedy expression on his face. Mary unwrapped the chocolate and broke off a few squares, giving some to Qasim and some to Hameed. Qasim grabbed his pieces quickly, as if he feared Hameed might snatch them from his hands. Then he stuffed all the squares into his mouth at once. Hameed glared at him furiously.

"Why can't we take this gentleman along with us?

He seems to be a friend of yours, after all, from the way you're acting with him."

Hameed, still holding the squares of chocolate in his hand, said angrily, "No, that won't be possible."

"Fine. As you wish."

"You are going to be pf-pushed down a well, do you hear me?" Qasim said, raising his finger in warning. Then his expression changed, and he opened his eyes wide, as if struggling against the onset of sleep. Suddenly, Mary rose from her chair. "Let's go," she said.

But Qasim remained motionless. It seemed that he had been suddenly overpowered by drowsiness. Hameed noticed that Mary was acting somewhat anxious. He felt a quiet pinch of suspicion. As they stepped out to the cloakroom and Hameed collected his coat from the coat-check girl, he cast a look back through an open window at Qasim, out of the corner of his eye. Qasim had fallen fast asleep leaning back in his chair. Hameed was still holding the pieces of chocolate in his hand. He dropped them into his jacket pocket.

Turning toward the exit, he smiled and remarked casually, "Good riddance. I was starting to think it would be difficult to get away from that gigantic fool."

"Y-yes," Mary said, apparently startled to hear Hameed's voice. "Yes... I've never seen a giant like him. So tall and so broad!"

"Indeed, he is unusual in every way. Let's go."

• • •

Doctor Dread was pacing furiously, like a beast in a cage. He was no longer in the same building where he had spent the night. This was a small room, with steel cabinets lining its walls. There was no other furniture.

The Doctor opened one of the cabinets. There was a

concealed phone in it. He dialled a number and began to shout, in a voice as loud as a trumpeting elephant: "Who is this? What are you fellows doing out there? Send Craig in."

He put down the receiver, closed the cabinet, and resumed pacing as before.

A minute later, there was a knock, then a curtain was parted and a man entered.

"What's the news?" the Doctor asked, fixing the man with his eye like a bloodthirsty animal.

"Everything is okay, sir. Mary will certainly bring them here. The report a minute ago was that they had left the Maypole."

"But where is Faridi?"

"I think he must be watching the two of them."

"He won't necessarily be duped into following them here. Learn to use your brain, Craig."

"Sir, I'm certain that Captain Hameed has told him about Mary's invitation. But Faridi isn't as stupid as Hameed. He'll assume that Hameed is walking into a trap, and then it's likely that he'll come here himself hoping to spring it."

The Doctor made a face. "You're being naïve. You don't realize what sort of man we're dealing with this time. Be that as it may, before two days are up, I want to see the dead bodies of both Faridi and Finch."

"We're doing our best, sir."

"And this is your best? Sending that stupid woman out on this mission?" the Doctor asked caustically.

"We try to follow your example, sir."

There was a sharp note of insubordination in Craig's voice, and the Doctor heard it. He stared at him in surprise.

"I am not wrong, sir," Craig answered boldly. "I know

that you are a lover of justice, so you'll let me live, despite my sarcastic comment."

"Yes, I believe in just treatment," Dread growled angrily. "State what you mean."

"Don't you ever make mistakes yourself?"

"Yes, very rarely, I do. But then I always take steps to correct them immediately."

"But there must have been times when you have failed to take corrective action quickly enough."

"I've had about enough of this. Explain yourself," the Doctor snarled.

"When Mary Singleton had already committed a mistake once, why make the same mistake again? I'm talking about the incident with the poisoned needle. Why was the same kind of needle used on that crime reporter Anwar at Begum Irshad's house? Especially when Faridi had made sure the first incident was so widely publicized?"

Doctor Dread's growl turned to laughter. The laughter went on for so long that Craig began to be frightened, and soon he was trembling badly.

The Doctor went silent suddenly, as if a machine had been switched off. Then he boomed, "Do you think I'm a fool? That was no mistake. It was my strategy. What do you know about that woman, Begum Irshad? I've not seen many others like her. She does not scare easily—in fact, she fears nothing except the law. Therefore, I thought it would be appropriate to make the police take an interest in her. I knew that *that* would finally make her lose her poise... and I would get to see if she was really the stone-tough politician she pretends to be. Her warning to Anwar was meaningless; what could *he* ever do to me? My plan was to make sure she was being assailed from all sides, so that she would be railroaded into meeting my demands. But see her, still roaming through the city's streets in her horse and carriage...."

"Yes, yes, sir. I... I see."

"Get out!" the Doctor exploded, pointing to the door.

Craig stepped backwards through the door, without turning around. Perhaps he believed that if he turned his back on the Doctor, death would jump up and pounce upon him.

The Doctor resumed his agitated pacing up and down the length of the room. Suddenly, he turned towards the door, startled. The yellow-cloaked angel's face was peeping out from behind the curtain.

"Tee-hee!" he giggled, his teeth showing. "May I come in?"

"Come," the Doctor growled, glaring at him.

"The moon will descend upon the earth at three o'clock this morning," he prophesied. After a few moments' silence, he went on, "Where is my moonbeam? Please, for God's sake, let them bring her here."

Dread smiled. "Not just one moonbeam. There are two!"

"Ahh, ahh!" the yellow-cloaked angel exclaimed, and began to jump up and down, beating his chest. With his long beard and yellow cloak, he looked truly bizarre.

The Doctor opened the phone cabinet and spoke into the phone. "Craig, send in Dolly and Mona. I'm in the mood for some entertainment."

"Aha! Dolly... and Mona!" the yellow-cloaked angel said, sucking his breath in through his teeth in pleasure.

The Doctor smiled, waiting.

A minute later, there was a knock on the door, and two young Caucasian women entered. Both wore short skirts, one orange and the other light blue. The Doctor pointed to the yellow-cloaked angel who stood silent and blinking. The two approached him.

"Hello darling!" they said in unison.

"Hee hee! The two of you are like my life, my soul. Come to me, come!" He spread his arms wide.

One of the girls stepped up toward him, opening her arms as if to embrace him. But the moment she came within arm's reach of the yellow-cloaked man and he tried to pull her to him, she gave him a resounding slap.

"Oh! Oh!" Bewildered, the yellow-cloaked angel staggered backward.

"What did you do that for, Mona? You mean person, you!" the other girl said. Pulling the yellow-cloaked angel toward her, she began to caress the cheek that had been slapped.

"You're the mean one!" said Mona. "What gives you the right to caress the face of my darling?"

"To hell with your darling!" said Dolly, and delivered a slap to the man's other cheek. The yellow-cloaked angel jumped back, stunned and struck dumb. Mona caught hold of him again, but he didn't try to free himself. He was looking at Dread with wonder.

"So, do you like these two moonbeams?" The Doctor smiled.

"Yes, they are very beautiful," the angel said in a choked voice. "But why do they keep hitting me?"

This time Mona walked around and kicked the angel in the small of his back. He fell on his face. Now Dolly came into action. She didn't allow him to get up. Straddling his back, she began to caress his head.

The cabinet phone rang. The Doctor answered it, while the two moonbeams continued to knock the living daylights out of the angel.

"Yes? Craig? What's the matter?"

"There's a bit of a problem, sir," came the voice from the other end. "Captain Hameed didn't take the taxi. He drove away with the girl on his motorcycle."

"Stupid fools!" the Doctor growled. Then, turning to the girls—who had become noisy by then—he roared: "Take him away from here." Then he spoke into the phone again. "I warned you—but you're all just a bunch of cretinous fools. Did he take her to Faridi's residence?"

"Yes, Doctor, sir. Five and Eleven seek your permission to enter Faridi's house."

"Permission granted—if, that is, they want to be torn limb from limb by ferocious dogs."

"Then what should we do?" Craig sounded flustered; in fact, he was at his wit's end.

The Doctor thought for a moment. "Now... we must let things take their own course."

"And the girl?"

"I am finished with her. I won't be sorry if she must be disposed of... But wait. Does she know this place, where I am now?"

"No, Doctor."

"Fine. Then forget about her." The Doctor's voice became softer. "But you must listen carefully to the plan that I shall now reveal regarding Finch. He's staying at Spring Cottage. Listen, how many local men do you have with you now?"

"At the moment, I have eight."

"Good. Administer the Golden Scorpion injection to two of them. They should also be armed with two loaded pistols. Then use the same old trick! Drop them off in front of Spring Cottage, and you guys stay outside, hidden from view. After the incident, Finch won't stay inside. The moment he comes out, finish him off whichever way you can. But if this plan of mine fails on account of your laziness, then... You understand me, don't you? I won't tolerate two failures in one night!

"But what if he's not there in the cottage?"

"Then do nothing."

"But then the lives of two of our men will have gone to waste!" the voice at the other end protested.

"Stop sniveling!" the Doctor growled. "That's nothing. *Thousands* of lives have been sacrificed for the benefit of my experiments."

The Escape

The motorcycle turned into Faridi's driveway. Mary Singleton, riding the pillion, said in great alarm, "What is this place? Where have you brought me?"

Hameed said: "Oh, I thought I should let you see where I live." The motorcycle was by now driving up to the portico.

"No, No! I don't want to be here!" She looked around, her eyes full of terror. She jumped down from the bike.

"Fine, don't stay here then." Hameed smiled. "But I won't walk you back to the gate."

"What do you mean?"

"I mean them," he said, pointing to his right, where a pack of ten fierce-looking bloodhounds stood panting, their red tongues hanging out. "The moment you leave my side, those dogs will start howling in praise of your looks. They have a special fondness for pretty girls."

"Oh, I'm done for, utterly done for!" she wailed. "Even you have cheated me!"

"Never, my darling! I adore you. Come with me." Hameed said, and catching hold of her arm, began to drag her to the front verandah.

"What are you doing? I'll start screaming!"

"Go ahead and scream. No one will dare step inside to help you. Here, our word is law." Saying this, he half-dragged, half-pulled Mary onto the verandah, where Faridi was sitting, watching them in surprise.

"We came here straight from the church," Hameed said, sounding deferential. "Now you should bless us."

"What's that?"

"First, I looked for a mullah who would conduct the marriage as per our custom. Failing to find one, we were obliged to have a civil ceremony."

"Everything this gentleman claims is false," Mary said hurriedly, in an anxious voice. "He brought me here by force."

"Ha! What's that you say, darling?" Hameed said. "But I can produce our marriage certificate. No court will refuse to accept it as genuine!"

Hameed produced from his pocket the squares of chocolate that Mary Singleton had given him, and went on, "Here's your certificate of marriage to me. Your former husband, of course, is still lying unconscious in the Maypole." He pushed her towards an empty chair. "Now sit here quietly."

"What's the story?" Faridi asked softly.

Hameed began recounting the facts from the beginning. He spoke in Urdu, so Mary could not understand. The colour had drained from Mary's face, and she was looking very anxious.

After a moment's thought, Faridi said, "And you went to the rendezvous without keeping me informed?"

"Yes. That was a mistake, certainly."

"No. You did well. Nothing different would have happened if you had told me about it. Dread made a rotten move this time."

"What do you mean? I don't get it."

"It should be clear: he believed that after you received Singleton's invitation, I would send you off alone to meet her, and then I would watch you and follow you in secret.

Dread's men, in turn, would be watching and trailing *us*. That way, we would have been sure to get trapped in some sticky situation. Dread shouldn't have been stupid enough to imagine that I would jump blindly into a well, but it seems he was."

Then he turned to the girl, who was sitting quietly in her chair, and said, "I want to know one thing—then I won't ask you anything else. Just tell me who it was that you were so afraid of, that night when you pricked Hameed with the poisoned needle."

"But I've already told the Captain: there was an enemy gang there."

"Why are you carrying those drugged chocolates?"

"Oh, I see! You suspect me because of those!" Mary Singleton smiled. "I think I made a mistake, offering them to that big fellow. He fell into a deep sleep and couldn't come with us. He had been arguing with Captain Hameed... The truth is, sir, I suffer from insomnia. I keep these chocolates with me so that I can use them if I'm unable to sleep."

"Turn her to over to me, please," said Hameed. "I'll get the real story out of her."

But Faridi paid no attention to him. He spoke to Mary again. "Answer me truthfully. Who was it that you were afraid of, that night?"

"I don't know what you mean... you're reading too much into everything. I... I'm not feeling well."

"*I* will make you well," Hameed said. Mary did not reply.

"I assume the Doctor's men have you under surveillance," Faridi said, "but please don't think that they'd be able to set foot inside this house. Twice already I've gotten the better of Dread. If he had the capability to kill me, I'd have been found dead in my own bed by now. He's well aware that isn't New Mexico, or Texas, or Kansas, or Oklahoma."

Mary Singleton stared at him wordlessly. Her face now betrayed fear. Suddenly Faridi said, "Escort her to the gate."

"Why?" Hameed asked in surprise.

"I just want Dread, dead or alive—and besides one or two of his cronies, no one knows his whereabouts."

"This girl must know."

"I highly doubt it."

"So?" Hameed turned to Mary. "Tell us where we can find Dread. You might even be let off the hook."

"I don't understand what you're talking about."

"Take her to the gate and leave her there," Faridi spoke loudly and sternly. "Don't waste your time and mine."

Hameed was terribly upset at the idea of letting Mary go. Still, having no choice, he got up, and said to Mary in a choked voice, "Come along." But for some reason Mary was now acting even more frightened. She remained where she was.

"Why don't you just get up and come along?" Hameed said, irritated.

"No! I won't go." Her voice was trembling.

"What now, do I have to find a camel cart for her?" Hameed asked Faridi, striking his forehead in mock despair.

Faridi said nothing. He had become engrossed in a book, as if the whole matter was of no importance. Hameed turned to Mary again.

"Come, for God's sake. Come on."

"No! I won't go. I'd rather commit suicide right here than go out like that."

"Well, those mobsters won't be brave enough to come inside. It won't be easy for them to try and retrieve one of their people from this place," Faridi said, without taking his eyes away from his book.

"It isn't possible," Mary mumbled, "to deceive someone who knows so much."

Hameed gave Faridi a flustered and questioning look. He was unable to understand anything of what was going on.

"So you've realized that it's in your best interest to answer all my questions truthfully," Faridi said, his eyes still on the page.

"Yes, I am willing to answer your questions," Mary said with obvious sincerity.

Hameed gave a crow like a rooster, rubbed his head in frustration, and flopped back into a chair.

"So? Who were you afraid of that night?"

"Finch and his gang."

"Were they there at the Maypole?"

"Yes. Or so we suspected."

"Was Finch there too?"

"Yes, he was."

"But Finch can be easily identified by his size, even among thousands of people, isn't that so?"

"Somehow he's able to make himself taller."

"Quite right. And I know how he does it."

"Please," Hameed cut in, "tell me how he does it, or I'll start braying like a donkey."

"He's spent a lifetime working in circuses," Faridi said. "Haven't you ever seen circus clowns walk on stilts? They not only walk—some of them can sprint on those stilts, with surprising speed. Finch is a master of the art. He possesses artificial legs of different sizes which he uses to increase or diminish his height."

"You are quite right, sir," said Mary Singleton. "That's what the Doctor says, too. But I find it really hard to believe. His walk looks completely natural."

"Indeed, he is a true master of the art," Faridi said. After a moment's pause, he asked, "Do you know the reason why they are at each other's throats?"

"I think you must know the reason yourself, sir."

"Yes, I do know. I learned it just today, and I want confirmation from you."

"Finch was bringing up an orphan girl. He had trained her for the circus, and treated her as his own flesh and blood. One night, one of the Doctor's men abducted her from the circus. The next morning, her body was found in the street."

"And she was only thirteen years old?"

"Yes, that also is correct." Mary was weeping. She said in a choked voice, "Dread is a beast. I hate him. But none of the girls caught in his snare can ever get away from him, no matter what they do."

"Still, you have been spying on Finch and his men for him. Haven't you?"

"Yes, I did spy on Finch and his gang. But I sympathize with him deeply. In spite of that, I have been working against him. Just today, I informed the Doctor that Finch is staying at Spring Cottage."

"Where?" Faridi gave her a piercing look.

"At Spring Cottage. I would never have reported it to Dread, except that one of his men was with me at the time."

"What was your plan for now?"

"I was supposed to take Captain Hameed to a house in Arjun Pura. I don't know anything else. I took out the wrong chocolate by mistake. The plan was that I would come out of the hotel with Captain Hameed, where there would be a taxi waiting, driven by one of our men. I was supposed to give the drugged chocolate to the Captain after we boarded the taxi. But things went wrong. The

Captain flatly refused to leave his bike there. He said we should go to Arjun Pura on the bike, or not at all."

"At what time did you report to Dread about Finch, and what was your mode of communication?"

"I used my transmitter, because Dread changed his location last night."

"Where was he last night?"

In reply, Mary gave him the address of the diplomatic building where the body had been discovered that morning.

"So where is he now?" Faridi asked.

"Why would I have to use the radio transmitter if I knew where he was?"

"Fine. What do you want now?"

"Anything, as long as you don't send me outside."

Faridi ordered Hameed, "Take her up to one of the rooms on the third floor."

Hameed went upstairs with Mary Singleton and returned about twenty minutes later. He glanced at his watch and said, "I'll be dead in ten minutes."

"Why?"

"Cardiac arrest," Hameed said cheerily. "That is, unless you tell me why the threat to send her out worked so well."

"It's quite simple, really," Faridi said with a smile. "The police in America made several unsuccessful attempts to capture Dread by turning one of his own people against him and using him as a mole. But every time any member of Dread's mob was arrested, the man would be found dead soon after the police set him free. Dread's rule is that once any of his henchmen have been captured by the police and then released, he can't allow them to continue to exist."

"So what should we do with this girl, now? Pickle her in a jar, or preserve her like fruit?"

"Get up. Let's go have a little stroll around Spring Cottage."

"And what if she escapes?"

"If she tries it, you'll see her fate for yourself when we return."

• • •

Two figures entered the somewhat narrow gate of Spring Cottage. The whole of the front garden was lit up, as bright as day. There was a watchman stationed at the verandah; seeing two men enter the grounds, he moved quickly toward them. But they did not come towards the verandah. Instead, they made a left turn, hugging the cottage's compound wall. The guard, seeing this, bent low, took out his gun, and stepped out toward them.

There was a hedgerow of begonias planted at a distance of three or four feet from the boundary wall. The guard hid behind the hedge, keeping his eye on the two intruders, who were bending close to the wall as though looking for something.

One of the intruders shined a small flashlight at a spot in the wall and said to his companion, "I found the way."

"Where?" his companion asked eagerly.

"Here, just look!" With his finger, he pointed his finger to a hole in the wall.

"Aha! Then let's go, you first."

"No, you go first."

"What's that you say? *You* must go first."

"Don't waste time with this pointless argument. Go!"

"No, I'll never go first. The one who discovered the way in should take the first step."

The guard kept watching them in surprise, wondering what they were up to.

"Will you move now, or do I have to resort to other means?"

"And what means do you propose to resort to? Let's see!" The other man appeared to be enraged, for the hidden watcher saw him produce a gun. Then the other one drew a gun of his own, and they stood there with their gun barrels pointing at each other.

"You wouldn't dare!" one of them said.

"Why wouldn't I? You think I'm weaker than you?" the other cried. Then both fired simultaneously at each other. The man watching from behind the hedge got up and sprinted back toward the building. He dashed in blindly, but luckily managed to draw to a halt at the last moment, or else he would have collided with the diminutive man who was just then running out the door from inside the house.

"I'm very sorry, sir," said the guard, taking a couple of stumbling steps back.

"What happened? What is it?" The tiny man glared at him.

The watcher narrated the whole story quickly and briefly, his breath coming in short gasps. The tiny man put up a hand in warning.

"Danger!" he said. "Look, don't try to go back outside. Close all the doors. This could be a trap laid by the police."

"But sir, they fired at each other. I saw both of them fall in a heap."

"So you saw them fall. Those guns might be theatrical toys, or they may have been firing blanks. Go inside and sit tight. I'm leaving this place. The police can't have any evidence against you."

The tiny man jumped out of a window, landing in a courtyard in the back. New sounds of gunfire came from the grounds. The watchman stood stock still for a few moments; then, moving quickly, he shut the front door and all the windows. There was more gunfire, and a few screams.

There were four other men in the building, all of them foreigners. They now came into the hall. One of them asked, "What is it? What's going on?"

The watchman again gave a brief account of the recent events, as two more shots were heard from outside. Then he repeated the instructions that the tiny man had given him.

"But why did he think it was the police?" one of the four men said. "Why would the police play this kind of a game? It's obvious... they're Dread's men."

Just then, a bullet shattered the glass of one of the windows.

"No, listen," another man said, as they retreated to one of the inner rooms. "The Doctor's men couldn't possibly keep firing for so long, so openly, and in a public neighbourhood like this. I think it must be the police. We should get rid of all the weapons in the place."

They all gathered inside a large room and put their revolvers on a table. One of them collected the guns and wrapped them in a piece of cloth. The shooting was still going on outside, and now a furious knocking began on the front door.

"Hurry," one of them said, and lifting the bundle of guns, he walked out fast to the back door. He opened the door a crack and peered out. Having made sure there was no one there, he flung the bundle of weapons over the back wall with a powerful swing of his arm. There was no habitation on that site of the house, only green fields stretching far into the distance. Perhaps it was for these bucolic surroundings that the house had been given the name "Spring Cottage".

He came back to the central room. The pounding at the door had not stopped.

One of the men pulled a face and said, "My friend, what will we do if it *isn't* the police, now that you've made us get rid of our weapons?"

"Open the door," someone roared from outside.

All five men crept toward the front door. One of them asked in a deep voice:

"Who is it?"

"Police!" came the answer. "Open the door!"

"How do we know you're the police? A minute ago, there were robbers on the grounds. They were trying to loot the place."

"Don't think you can escape through the back, either. The house is surrounded from all sides."

"What a load of shit this is!" the man with the deep voice grumbled, loud enough to be heard through the door. "It seems impossible to come to this country and make it back home in one piece!"

"We're breaking down the door," the voice shouted loudly from outside, and the door began to be pounded so hard that it seemed it would not hold up much longer.

"Wait, wait, I'll open it," one of the five said, and advanced towards the door.

"No," another said. "Let them break it down. Suppose they're the same robbers that were firing in the grounds just now to frighten us?"

"There are two corpses out here," the voice said from outside. "You'll have to answer for them."

"We don't know anything about it. They can't be our men—all of us are here."

The vigourous assault on the door continued. The five occupants of Spring Cottage did nothing but watch quietly. The one who had suggested opening the door looked extremely anxious. Finally, the door gave way. Faridi called out loudly, gun in hand, "Police! This is a warning. Stay where you are, or none of you will survive."

They froze. "Put your hands up!" Faridi commanded. All five obeyed without protest.

Accompanying Faridi were Hameed and three other policemen. "Stay here," Faridi told them, and rushed into the building.

"We *are* being robbed, after all," one of the five said in a shaky voice.

Hameed flashed his card and said softly, "Well, my friends, where's Finch?"

"Finch? What Finch?" one of them, sounding surprised. "We don't know any Finch."

"Fine," Hameed said. "Stay here. Don't move." Turning to the policemen, he ordered, "Search these men."

Another among the five said, "Sir, we don't know what you want from us. We're the ones who were attacked by robbers—and here you are, a police officer, harassing innocent victims!"

"Shut up," Hameed snarled. "Search them thoroughly," he repeated to the policemen.

Faridi returned soon. He stared hard at the five men, then smiled and said, "So Finch made a clean getaway. And it will be hard for the police to bring any serious charges against you. Isn't that right? What do you say?"

"We don't understand what this is all about, sir."

"There are two men lying dead outside."

"I may be able to tell you something about them," the guard said. "But I'm not sure you'll believe me."

"Let me hear it first. Then I'll decide if I should believe you or not."

The guard then recounted to Faridi everything he had seen the two intruders do, from the time they entered the grounds of Spring Cottage. When he was done, Hameed burst out laughing. There was no change, however, in Faridi's serious expression. He asked, "Was Finch here at the time?"

The guard, who had been thrown off by Hameed's sudden laughter, spoke without thinking. "Yes," he said, but then quickly recovered. "What did you say, sir?"

"Nothing. Just tell me this much—where would Finch have gone from here?"

"Sir, please explain what you mean by this name 'Finch'. We have no idea who this person is."

"Place all five of them under arrest," Faridi directed Hameed. "To be sure, they'll have foreign passports, but there are two unexplained corpses on the grounds of their residence. We can keep them in custody at least until the matter is cleared up."

"Sir," one the men protested, "this is absolutely unjust and unwarranted treatment!"

"What is unwarranted about it?" Faridi said, fixing him with a stare. "Are suspects in your country ever set free without an investigation? You people will lock this house up and get into the police car without further protest. There have been two murders here, and you people have made contradictory statements."

"No we didn't!"

"First you said that you were attacked by robbers. Then, on further questioning, you came up with that unbelievable story."

"You must believe me," said the guard. "I saw the whole thing with my own eyes. The moment the two intruders fell, I ran back into the house. Then there was the sound of more gunshots, and we closed our door."

Faridi glowered at them and said, "Whatever. I still can't let you go without further investigation."

The building was locked up within a few minutes, and Faridi was on his way to the police station along with the five suspects. A policeman was left behind to guard the two dead bodies. Faridi returned to Spring Cottage shortly, having entrusted the suspects to the nearest police station.

"How is it that you treat Doctor Dread's men so benevolently, always letting them go, but you're not nearly so large-hearted with Finch's gang?" Hameed asked. "The fact is, I'm starting to get a sneaking feeling of sympathy for that little shrimp. And I think maybe you should feel the same way."

Faridi was silent for a moment. Then he said, "I only let the Doctor's men off when I'm certain that they're totally ignorant of the Doctor's real identity and whereabouts."

"Well, as of now, the Doctor's men made a clean getaway."

"Er, yes... I slipped up just a bit. When I heard the sound of gunfire, I determined that the game was afoot. Had I waited just a little longer, none of them could have got away."

"Are you absolutely sure that Finch and his people know where the Doctor is?"

"Well, Finch was here not too long ago. He escaped by scaling the back wall and jumping down. I saw his footprints there in the dirt."

"Those two bastards have been a real pain in the ass for a long time now," Hameed muttered. Then he saw Faridi suddenly jump across the hedgerow of begonias. Instinctively, Hameed was about to jump too, but then was shocked into immobility, and stood rooted to the ground. For he saw a tiny man spring up and begin scaling the wall with astounding agility. If the grounds had been just a little less brightly lit, he would have sworn that it was a monkey, and not a human being.

Faridi fired a shot, but the short time it took him to draw his gun was enough for the agile man to disappear.

"Run!" Faridi shouted, racing towards the gate. Hameed was right after him.

The Blue Bag

By the time they made it out across the lawn, through the gate, and behind the compound wall that Finch had jumped over, Hameed had lost hope that they would still be able to catch sight of him. But it seemed that Finch was just a bit too slow, or perhaps simply out of luck; for Faridi still caught a glimpse when they rounded the corner. At that very moment, Finch made a long leap into the wild shrubbery that marked the beginning of open, fallow land.

Faridi and Hameed ran at top speed, but when they cleared the shrubbery, they found that Finch had made an even longer leap across a gulch. Now they had lost the element of surprise.

Then Faridi caught hold of Hameed's hand and said, "Stop."

Baffled, Hameed stopped. But, when he looked up, he saw that Finch was standing still on the far side of the gulch. He could clearly see his silhouette framed against the starlight. Hameed aimed his pistol, but Faridi whispered, "No."

Hameed was furious. "But I finally have a chance to finish him! You're delaying for no reason!"

"He's a brave man, dear Captain, very daring and very intrepid. I wouldn't like to kill him like this."

"No? Then go ahead, have him over for cocktails if you want," Hameed sputtered. "It makes no difference to me!"

"Come on! Why don't you chase me?" came a mocking voice from across the gulch. "I haven't run a good footrace for years. Now there's a chance for one, but you two are dragging your feet!"

"Do you hear that?" growled Hameed. "That son of a flea is challenging us!"

Faridi laughed softly. Hameed's temper went up another notch. "If you weren't in the Criminal Investigation Department, the only other place for you would be the loony-bin."

"You're quite correct," Faridi said softly, and fell silent.

Finch stayed where he was.

"What the...?" Hameed suddenly exclaimed loudly in surprise. Three or four men had appeared as if from nowhere and launched an attack on Finch.

"Are they your people?" Hameed asked, pulling at Faridi's sleeve.

"No... no," Faridi replied. There was a trace of worry in his voice. Then he took out his gun and fired into the air. The shot seemed to stun Finch's assailants for a moment, for their hands stopped moving. Then they bounded off into the low-lying field below. Now they were no longer visible to Faridi and Hameed.

They heard three screams, one after the other. Faridi moved quickly into the gulch; Hameed tried to follow suit, but he got entangled in the thorny underbrush and fell on his face. By the time he pulled himself free of the brambles, Faridi was no longer in his field of vision. He rose and started running, ignoring all his cuts and bruises, and climbed over to the other side of the gulch with a speed that he himself was amazed at.

But he found only Faridi on the other side, who said, "That makes five, in all."

"Five? Five what?" Hameed panted.

"Bodies," Faridi answered briefly. Then Hameed noticed the three men who lay collapsed on the ground.

"They're dead?" he asked in bewilderment.

"Yes."

"But... but you fired in the air."

Faridi reprimanded him tersely, "Where the hell are your brains?"

Hameed bent down to examine the bodies.

"They have been knifed to death," Faridi said, "and the killer was phenomenally skilled with the weapon. The victims couldn't have lasted more than a minute; the knife cut straight into their hearts."

"But who are they?"

"The Doctor's minions, who else?"

"My God! So it was Finch who killed them! And still you let him go!"

"What the hell do you mean, I let him go?"

"Well, if you hadn't insisted on waiting, and we'd gone after him when we had the chance, then we—"

"Then we wouldn't have come out alive. The Doctor's men had concealed themselves there among the overgrown shrubs, ready to ambush Finch. You couldn't have averted their attack any more than you could change the direction of an arrow shot at you in the dark. I, for one, can't claim to be able to survive a stealth attack. So I'd say that my habit of keeping a cool head saved me by a hair's breadth."

Hameed said nothing. He was considering what would have happened if he had been alone. He never would have been able to resist the temptation of going after Finch, and would probably have met the very fate that Faridi had just avoided. He didn't want to think too much about exactly what that fate would have been.

"In fact," Faridi went on, "I believe this fellow Finch

is far more dangerous than the Doctor. And I have never been wrong before."

Hameed was still wordless, looking as if he had stepped on a snake. Faridi continued his monologue. "It's no use thinking of giving chase. By now there won't even be a trail of dust left. He could have made himself scarce if he wanted; I wonder why he came back to Spring Cottage... Wait! Yes, why did he return, after all? Perhaps he forgot something valuable he had left behind there, and had to come back to retrieve it!"

Faridi had become unusually animated. Now he now addressed Hameed directly. "Come on, hurry, hurry! Don't you see why he came back, what his purpose was in challenging us? He must have wanted to give us the runaround, so that he could re-enter the cottage while we were wasting our time in pursuit!"

They ran back to Spring Cottage, stumbling quickly through the gulch. It seemed to Hameed that his brain had frozen. He'd stopped thinking about anything at all; what could he do, anyway? The situation kept changing with astonishing speed.

Faridi found the policeman stationed where he had left him.

"Did anyone come this way?" he asked.

"No, sir."

"Let's go," Faridi said to Hameed. Then, turning to the policeman, Faridi said, "Don't let anyone enter the compound—whether it's a regular citizen or a government official."

"Yes, sir," he said with a salute, and proceeded towards the gate on the double.

"But you had them lock the door," Hameed mumbled. "And we don't have the keys."

"That's one of the reasons I sent that constable to the gate. I'll have to pick the lock."

Faridi stepped onto the verandah and switched the lights off. Hameed knew that the lock would present no trouble for Faridi, who always carried a set of housebreaking tools with him.

Within a minute or so, they were back inside the house.

• • •

Doctor Dread was snarling like a wounded wolf. Craig stood before him, shaking like an aspen leaf, as if the very next moment would be his last.

"I'll have you all put to death!"

Trembling all over, Craig said, "The great Doctor... believes in justice."

"Yes, and it's justice that I'll give you."

"Please, Doctor, please listen to what I'm saying. We would have put an end to Finch today, except that blasted fellow Faridi jumped in and surprised us."

"Again, it was your fault that he jumped in. And for that you must be punished."

"Why was it my fault, Doctor?"

"Because Mary Singleton knew that Finch was in Spring Cottage."

"But how could I have known that she knew?"

"Why did you cook up that scheme without consulting me? Yes, you are right. I do love justice. And it is justice you'll get."

The hidden phone in the cabinet started ringing. Dread turned to answer it, leaving Craig to consider his fate.

"Who is it?" he barked into the phone.

"Sam speaking, Doctor, sir."

"Yes?"

"It's that blue bag you were interested in. It's not there in the box."

"What nonsense! Look again."

"Please listen. Instead of the bag, there was a card-board box bearing the inscription: *A present from Finch, for Doctor Dread.* The box contains a rotten potato."

"No! How did that bastard Finch get access to the box?" Doctor Dread shouted into the phone.

"Craig should be the one to answer that question. He's been getting very careless of late. He's always running after that Dolly. They were back at their noisy antics just a little while ago."

"Does this mean Finch knows about this hideout, too?"

"Given the facts, I don't think we can escape that conclusion."

"Okay." The Doctor disconnected the line and turned to Craig. What he saw then was rather unexpected. Craig's unsteady hands now held an automatic. Although the gun was pointing towards the Doctor, Craig was barely able to control his shaking.

"Now there will be no justice possible, Doctor." His voice was trembling.

"No, there won't," the Doctor smiled. "But take a look at your hands. You think you can really manage to pull the trigger? I do appreciate your audacity, though. It's not an easy thing to aim a gun at Doctor Dread. I shall reward your courage by forgiving you. As a further reward, I will also let you have Dolly."

Craig was open-mouthed.

"I don't want to waste the few good men that remain with me. Otherwise, I'd be left quite alone," Dread said gently. "But from now on, you must be more careful in whatever you do."

"I w-w-will," Craig stammered. "I'll be very careful, D-Doctor, sir."

"Good. Otherwise, even one misplaced step will ruin

us all. Well, okay... now there's only one plan left to be set into motion for Finch. Open the third cabinet from the left. Take out the tube filled with red fluid."

Craig put his gun back in its holster and stepped forward to the cabinet like an obedient servant. He opened it and looked carefully for the tube in the upper shelf.

"Yes, sir. Here it is, the tube of red fluid." Holding the tube gingerly, he turned toward the Doctor and showed him the tube.

"Fine.... Now give it a good shake, and examine it against the light. See whether there are white particles floating free in the red fluid."

Craig shook the tube vigorously, brought it close to his face, and examined it against the light. A second later, the tube burst with a small popping sound, and the red liquid splashed onto Craig's face.

"Aaaa! Aargh!" Craig bellowed like a wild buffalo and fell to the floor with a thud. His hands were clawing at his eyes, and he was screaming and writhing in pain and terror. "You murdered me! You swine! You vicious dog!" Curses poured from his mouth as he writhed and rolled in agony. Dread stood above him, cold and motionless, a cruel smile on his lips. Craig continued screaming his life away. The Doctor's eyes now shone with an evil light of pleasure, the look of someone watching their favourite sport. Craig's screams became fainter as the minutes passed. Finally, with a spasm, his head slumped to one side and he went still. Both his eyes had been melted into pools of viscous liquid.

"Dread's justice," he muttered, and turned away from the body. Picking up his hidden phone, he spoke urgently into it: "Sam? Is that you? Listen, we have to vacate this building immediately. Move to Number Three. All our hard work will be wasted if the blue bag isn't found. Now Finch must die at any cost. He has learned about this location, too. It's possible that he may lead the police here, and I don't want to confront the police before I have settled the matter of Irshad's widow.... You have a soft spot for Dolly, don't you?"

"N-no, sir."

"I know you fancy her. She is hereby yours—a gift, in recognition of your loyal services."

"But... But sir, Craig will become my sworn enemy!"

"Craig..." He turned to look at the contorted, tortured body. "I regret to inform you that Craig is no longer among the living. He died as the result of a small misadventure while testing a tube of Nine/Three. The tube burst in his hand. In any case, you must immediately organize a move to Number Three. Understand?"

"Yes. Yes, sir." The voice at the other end was choked, as if the speaker was having difficulty enunciating. The Doctor put the phone down.

• • •

Faridi and Hameed began a thorough search of Spring Cottage. They went about the job with great caution, using their torches rather than switching on any of the lights.

Hameed did not have his heart in the job at all. Had Faridi not been there, Hameed would have made himself scarce. It wasn't that he was being cowardly; in fact, the thought that a bullet might come tearing out of the darkness at any moment to shatter his skull didn't really bother him at all. It was just that he was fed up. It was part of his nature to get fed up easily, and when things didn't turn out the way he expected, he got even more fed up.

He had thought that tonight would be the night they would finally arrest Finch. Yet, contrary to his hopes, the little insect had eluded all efforts toward his capture. To cap it all off, Finch's final challenge had been particularly galling; it made Hameed feel mentally exhausted. *Just imagine!*—he fumed to himself—*How could a puny little fellow like that, not more than four-and-a-half feet tall, mock and challenge a man like Faridi, and get away with it?* Hameed felt like shooting Faridi dead for having tarnished his international reputation in such a manner.

The truth was that Hameed was just as prone to hero-worship as any other human being. He hated to see any flaws or shortcomings in the greatness of his most revered hero.

He moved around the house listlessly, pretending to help with the search. Finally, Faridi himself asked him, "What's wrong with you? You seem listless."

"Yes, sir. I've just witnessed a courageous man getting his face rubbed in the dirt."

Faridi smiled. "You fool! Who do you think I am, Tarzan? Or maybe the son of *Hunterwali*?"

"Maybe it means nothing to you. But I feel like committing suicide."

"No, no, not here!" Faridi said in mock horror. "We already have five bodies to get rid of."

Faridi's torchlight moved slowly about, piercing into nooks and corners. Suddenly, Hameed saw the torch drop from Faridi's hand. He leapt toward the door.

"The light! Hameed, the light!" Faridi whispered, and jumped out the door.

Hameed bent down to pick up the fallen torch, but he kept going down, until his face was pressed to the floor. Someone had tackled him and then run off.

Faridi called from outside of the room: "It's Finch, I saw him! Finch—there's no way out of the room now."

Hameed rose quickly. Knowing that Finch was in the room with him, he hugged the wall, taking advantage of the near-total darkness. Having been unable to retrieve Faridi's torch, he reached in his pocket for his own torch, and his other hand went to his shoulder holster for his automatic; but both hands came up empty. Apparently, he had lost both in the recent fall.

"Surrender to me, Finch!" Faridi called.

"Get away from the door, my friend," Hameed heard Finch saying. "Or else you'll have to pick up your friend's dead body as well. Do as I say and he won't come to any harm—I really don't have any quarrel with you two."

Hameed began a slow crawl in the direction of Finch's voice. The very next moment, he heard Faridi cry out. It sounded as if he was falling, but had controlled his fall.

"Stop, Finch! Or I'll shoot!"

Then Hameed heard the sound of running feet. He ran out of the room after the sound. He discovered that the back door of the building, which opened onto the fields outside and below, was open. He called out to Faridi, but there was no answer. He didn't know what to do next. All the options seemed to present a risk of one sort or another. Finally, he decided to stick to his position by the back door.

A minute later, Faridi reappeared in the doorway. Although it was quite dark, Hameed would never fail to recognize Faridi's silhouette, even in the faintest starlight.

"Hameed, look, there's a switchboard somewhere on the verandah. Turn the lights on. That little imp has literally slipped away from under my feet."

Hameed found the switch. Light flooded the backyard. He saw Faridi bend down and pick up something from the ground. Coming closer, he saw that it was a small blue leather bag.

"This is what he came back for. He was trying to run off with it," Faridi said, "but it fell from his grasp while he was climbing the wall. My God, how agile he is! Faster than a monkey. First, he hit my hand with a rock and forced me to drop my torch, and then he made off with the bag.... But listen, why couldn't you catch him? You had every opportunity this time."

Hameed made no reply. Faridi laughed softly and said, "Did you ever encounter such a criminal? I swear, sometimes I love these antics of his. What nerve he's got!"

A Tiny Packet of Mischief

Begum Irshad drew the window blinds, put on her nightdress, and moved towards her bed. She stopped when she heard the trill of the phone in the corner.

"Hello?" she yawned.

"Who's speaking?" said a voice from the other end.

"This is Begum Irshad."

"Good. This is Anwar speaking, ma'am."

"What is it?" Her tone was unexpectedly mild.

"I want to return the ten thousand rupees that Shaheena gave me."

"I have nothing to do with that money."

"Well, if I'm not working for Shaheena anymore—"

"Why aren't you working for her?" Begum Irshad interrupted him.

"I don't want to see her go on suffering those fits of madness."

"You go on investigating; do whatever you want. Just don't ever try to come here. And don't ever try to meet Shaheena either."

"Then what results can I hope to achieve, Begum Irshad? I don't even know the basic facts."

"I'll make you a new offer. Fifty thousand. You have to find a man."

"I'm ready."

"But the police mustn't come to know about it."

"Come to know about what?"

"That you're looking for him."

"Can do. As long as the job doesn't involve killing the person."

"No. His murder will not be required."

"And why is it so important to find this man?"

"You aren't being paid fifty thousand to know the reasons."

"Okay. I won't concern myself with your motives. But you'll at least have to give me a name and description."

"Name...? I don't remember his name. But he has a dark red mark on his right wrist—a mark the size of a rupee coin. You should look for him in Arjun Pura, or other slum areas of the city."

"That's all? Nothing else?"

"That's all I know about him."

"Then fifty thousand is too little, Begum Irshad. I'll have to roll up the sleeves of at least a million and a half men. Let's see, if you give me two annas per head, I might just become eligible to pay income tax."

"Are you making fun of me?" Begum Irshad asked angrily.

"No, ma'am, but this is a very difficult job. You yourself have been wandering around looking for this man for many nights now. Have *you* found any trace of him?"

"You are right. It is a difficult job. But I can't offer more than fifty thousand."

"For you, I can even do it for free... But wait. Why don't I go after your blackmailer instead, and grab *him* by the scruff of his neck?"

"My blackmailer?" Begum Irshad echoed with surprise. "Do you know him?"

"No. But it won't be hard to find him, if I try."

"Have you mentioned anything about this to Colonel Faridi?"

"No. But I did file a report against you."

"So that's why Colonel Faridi came here to make inquiries. Did you say anything in your report about someone blackmailing me?"

"Not at all. I was working on that case, how could I mention it? Shaheena paid me ten thousand to find your blackmailer. Then I filed the report against you to forestall any legal action by you against me."

"Well, let's forget all that. Now I'll say this: if you can trace that blackmailer, I'll pay you one lakh."

"You don't know him personally?"

"No. I have only heard his voice."

"And from his accent, he sounds like a foreigner."

"If you already know that, then you have just as much information about him as I do." Begum Irshad sighed deeply. "But remember, you may not step into my house until you have captured him."

"How much is he asking for?"

"Two crores."

"Dear God! Even a quarter of that would make me rich as Qaroon. How I wish *I* had something to blackmail you with!"

"Then go ahead. Join forces with him," Begum Irshad said bitterly.

Anwar laughed. "But you must have seen him—on the night of the birthday party, at least?"

"Though circumstances and events suggest that I might have seen him then, the fact is that I did not. I only received a letter from him—and the needle. I was obliged to do what the letter asked me to do. If I hadn't, I would have faced unspeakable ignominy and dishonour. He could have even asked me to kill you, and I wouldn't have refused."

"Thanks a lot."

"Imagine yourself in my shoes before you judge me."

"But you still won't tell me why you are being blackmailed?"

"No," she answered, curtly and sternly, and hung up the phone.

• • •

It was a large building, surrounded on all sides by fruit trees. Though constructed in a style that was no longer in vogue, the building still looked impressive.

None of the neighbours knew anything about any Westerner in residence there. None of them, looking at Doctor Dread in his present guise, would ever guess that he was anything other than a traditional Middle Eastern man, a lover of the older way of life. He sported a dark black beard and wore the customary Middle Eastern cloak, and occasionally wore a keffiyeh as well. Even the common people who lived in the shacks and the servants' quarters around the building believed he was a rich Arab. All his companions looked and dressed like Arabs as well. His women observed strict purdah. The building had been obtained on rent from a wealthy landowner from an old noble family.

It would not be wrong to say that Dread was obliged to go to these great lengths to conceal his identity because of Finch, and only Finch. Dread regarded the country's police—indeed, all the law enforcement in the whole world—as his playthings. And even though Faridi had twice gotten the better of him, he wasn't terribly afraid of Faridi, either.

But he feared Finch—feared and hated him. Even now, he was walking in his garden pondering the problem that Finch posed. If he had known where Finch was to be found, he would have taken every possible measure to destroy him—but he didn't. What was more, he couldn't be sure that Finch hadn't discovered *his* present location.

"Sam!" He addressed the man who was following closely behind him.

"Yes, Doctor?"

"How do you propose we sort out the problem of Finch?"

"All of us must work together, most industriously, to destroy him—or else he will destroy us. I see no other way."

"Now don't give that tiny insect more importance than he deserves. He's like an impudent crow that snatches the bone from under the wolf's nose. He is bent upon spoiling my business with Begum Irshad."

"But Doctor, please consider the fact that so far, he's been responsible for the deaths of fifteen of our very best men."

"Well, yes," he said carelessly. "That is, indeed, unfortunate." He put a cigarette to his lips and lit it.

"There is only one way to bring this business with Begum Irshad to a conclusion," he went on, drawing deeply on the cigarette. "We must kidnap her daughter, that which she loves above all else. Now that we have lost that blue bag, it's our only remaining option. We can do nothing else to her."

"That Finch fellow is like some evil spirit! It shouldn't have been humanly possible to steal that bag."

"No, there's nothing supernatural about it." The Doctor made a face. "It only happened because Craig was careless."

"Yes, that's true, too."

They fell silent. Dread became lost in thought again. He spoke after a few minutes. "No. That won't be right."

"What won't be right, sir?"

"Kidnapping the girl. It might complicate matters. Then again, I don't shy away from complications and difficulties... But Finch..."

Dread stopped. This was a pleasant garden grove; he often relaxed here on the green grass, enjoying the breeze and the light, sweet scent from the jasmine bushes that surrounded the trees. Dread leaned against a dead tree, the upper half of which had been sawn off, leaving a tall stump. The Doctor rested his elbows on it and crinkled his brow in concentration, not fully alert to his surroundings. As Sam looked around to make sure that the location was secure, the Doctor suddenly fell to the ground with a thud, the tree stump fallen across his chest.

With admirable presence of mind, Dread pushed the tree stump off his chest and moved quickly away. Then there was a shot, and the bullet barely missed his side. He leapt back further, but the stump was now rolling over the grass towards him. Dread pulled out his gun and let off three quick shots, but he either missed the rolling log, or else the bullets didn't penetrate the wood.

Sam was staring at the bizarre scene open-mouthed and wide-eyed.

"Sam! You stupid bastard! Don't you see?" the Doctor bellowed. "He's there, inside the hollow of the tree trunk! Don't just stand there gawking!"

Then, suddenly, Finch was in front of him. He emerged from the hollow stump as fast as a mouse scampering out of its hole. He fired twice at the Doctor. The first shot went wide; the second would have finished the Doctor forever—except that Sam sprang at Finch at the last minute, spoiling his aim. As Finch slipped through Sam's arms, he fired again. In the instant before the shot, Dread dropped to the ground, fooling Finch into thinking he had hit him.

Turning to Sam, Finch said, "Up with the hands!"

Sam looked despairingly at the Doctor. He lay huddled on the ground, face down and motionless.

Holding the gun with his right hand, Finch produced a knife from under his left sleeve, tossed it to the ground in front of Sam, and said:

"Cut off his nose and give it to me, so I can place it on that little girl's grave and try to ease the torment of her soul."

Sam bent down, picked up the knife, and approached Dread with trembling hands and uncertain steps. Dread was lying quite still. Finch also stepped forward, hoping to enjoy the sight of Dread's corpse being disfigured. But the very next moment he regretted having dropped his guard. For Dread was suddenly up again; Finch lost his gun, and found himself pinned under the Doctor's bulk.

"The knife, Sam! The knife!" Dread called out at the top of his lungs. "I'll slaughter him like a lamb!"

But then he bellowed like a wounded buffalo and fell to the side, letting Finch free. Sam blinked... but where was Finch? He turned and saw him leaping and bounding like a wild deer towards the compound wall. Sam gave chase, but long before he could get anywhere near him, Finch had reached the wall, scrambled up it like a monkey, and disappeared over the other side.

Sam had no choice but to stop. He knew that no one could outrun Finch. Also, just behind the wall, there was a jungle-growth of dense and thorny karonda shrubs. The building was ten miles from the city; there was hardly anything like a road nearby. Finch would be entirely uncatchable.

He returned with dejected steps to the grove where the Doctor sat, a look of acute pain on his face.

"You traitor!" He pointed a finger at Sam and spoke in a voice full of anger and pain. "You were about to cut off my nose, weren't you?"

"D-Doctor, sir, I thought you were d-d—"

"Dead!" the doctor shouted, but his voice was feeble. He groaned. His eyes were downcast; his head was slumped, and he was even finding it difficult to breathe. Then he raised his hand in entreaty, and said haltingly, "Now run.... Run from here, to the safe house. Quickly. Take me... inside."

He fell flat on the ground, groaning. The bewildered Sam ran to the house to get help.

• • •

Although Begum Irshad had specifically told him to keep out of Irshad Manzil, Anwar knew that it was absurd to believe that he could lay his hands on the blackmailer while staying completely away from the house. So he had taken extra care this time with his disguise, until he was sure that he was completely unrecognizable.

In fact, Anwar was now a permanent resident of Irshad Manzil. It so happened that Begum Irshad was inordinately fond of game meat. One of the hunters she employed had conveniently fallen sick, and Anwar came in as his replacement, without her even realizing who he was.

He would become especially alert whenever the Dunkitales showed their faces at the house. He realized that Roger, the elder Dunkitale, was trying to seduce Begum Irshad, and Hunter, the younger one, was playing the same game with Shaheena.

At the present moment, Hunter was walking in the grounds with Shaheena. Anwar, concealing himself, was able to hear their conversation easily. Hunter was saying:

"My father is a perfect fool. Even to this day, he hasn't learned the proper way to talk to women."

"Why don't you teach him?" Shaheena asked.

"Good Lord!" Hunter put his hands to his ears and made a face. "I'll never be able to teach him anything, unless he shaves off that moustache of his. Once, just a single hair from it somehow entered my nostril. I sneezed and sneezed. Daddy really is a perfect duffer, you see."

Shaheena's face showed her distaste for Hunter's nonsensical prattle, but she said nothing.

"Do you know what he said once, to the older sister of one of his female friends..." Before he could finish telling the joke, Hunter began to laugh. He controlled his mirth with some difficulty, and went on. "He was falling a little bit in love with that female friend, I think. So one day, her older sister—"

Shaheena was annoyed. "I don't want to hear anything about this older sister."

"Okay. I'll tell you about the female friend, then. That's an interesting story too."

Shaheena's temper rose even higher. She said sharply, "Did I ask you to come walk with me?"

"So, you're upset," he said in a voice laden with pathos. "What do you know..."

He put his hand on his breast and fell silent. The expression on his face was like someone suffering from tuberculosis.

"Are you in your right mind?"

"I wish I was. Ever since I laid eyes on you, I've been eating my lunch at dinnertime and my dinner at lunchtime. Often, I shave myself twice in a day. But when I come back to my senses, I find that I've actually been shaving my father. Then Daddy smiles, and thanks me."

"Hunter Dunkitale, stop blathering, or I'll call a servant to throw you out."

"Sure, sure," he said, "as long as he's better-looking than I am."

By now, Shaheena had by now lost both her temper

and her restraint. She struck him on the face with a powerful blow. The sound of the slap carried for some distance around them. Yet Hunter Dunkitale didn't rub his face where it hurt, nor did anything in his expression change to indicate that he'd just been smacked.

"*He* taught us," he said, raised a finger towards the sky, "that when one is slapped, one should turn the other cheek."

And indeed, Shaheena promptly slapped him a second time. Hunter took out his handkerchief and extended it toward her, saying: "Come, let me wipe your hands. My cheeks might have been dirty."

Shaheena said nothing. She turned away, as if she didn't care, and made for the house with long, resolute strides. Anwar noticed a cruel smile cross Hunter Dunkitale's lips.

The Night of Terror

Mary Singleton was like an entirely different person. She no longer wore Western clothes, preferring dresses that hid most if not all of her body, in fact favouring saris most of the time. She had stopped wearing any sort of make-up as well. She was still extremely attractive, but there was a world of difference in the Mary of the past and the Mary of the present. She had the look of someone who had been living chastely all her life.

Mary's transformation was a source of continual astonishment to Hameed every time he looked at her. What was more, she now spent most of her time reading the Bible, and if Hameed ever succeeded in striking up a conversation with her, she would use the occasion to tell him stories of the saints and martyrs.

But today, Hameed had finally cajoled her into talking to him and laughing at his jokes. She was giggling merrily, like a little girl, without a trace of affectation or flirtatiousness.

Hameed said, "I'm so very sad today, and yet here you are laughing away like crazy."

"Why are you sad?"

"I'm sad because I can't be a good person, like you are."

"What evil could there be in you?" she said, surprised. "You are neither a thief, nor a drunk, nor a womanizer."

"Nevertheless, my billy goat doesn't have a good opinion of me."*

She laughed, but then immediately became serious, and said, "No, you and the Colonel are both perfect angels! You are the first people in my life who didn't try to use me against my wishes. And generally speaking, I feel that the East hasn't yet fallen so morally low as the West."

"Thanks," Hameed answered with equal seriousness—for this matter concerned the dignity and sanctity of the East.

After some moments' silence, Hameed tried to steer the conversation in a different direction. "Still, it saddens me to think that you've been caught in the snare of fraudulent people like us."

"Why? Why fraudulent?" Mary gave a start, and stared at him.

"Why, isn't it a fraud what we're doing, giving you protective asylum just so we can lay our hands on Dread through you?"

"Through me?" Mary was surprised. She spoke again after a moment's silence. "I think you may be labouring under a misapprehension. The Doctor has about thirty-six different safe houses in this city. I only know nine of them, but Colonel Faridi knows of at least twenty-five. What help can I hope to offer such a man?"

"How do you know that the Colonel knows about at least twenty-five of Dread's hideouts?"

"He told me himself."

This was news for Hameed. He had no idea whatsoever

---

* Hameed's pet billy goat, Bhagra Khan, which he dresses in a tie and felt hat, is introduced in #39, *Andhaeray ka Shehenshah* ("Emperor of the Dark"). Faridi does not approve of the pet. – Ed.

of the extent of Faridi's information, or indeed of its source.

After a moment's thought, he asked, "How much do you know about that yellow-cloaked person who was in your care?"

"I just took care of him. I know nothing about him, except that he's mentally ill."

"What is his position among Dread's men?"

"I couldn't really say. I know this much—he's deranged in some way, and he is always drooling over women."

"What connection could he possibly have with Dread?"

"I don't know. I've seen him insult Dread to his face, but Dread just laughs at the crazy man's dirty words—it's quite out of character for the Doctor."

"You said that you sympathize with Finch."

"Yes, certainly."

"But don't you realize that he is a murderer many times over?"

"Maybe he is," she shrugged. "But he wasn't a murderer early in life. He used to live frugally and earn a livelihood through hard work, like any other honest man. He only strayed from the path of goodness in his obsession with getting revenge on Dread, and now he's become as bad a man as Dread himself. He robs others of their money without remorse, murders without regret. But you mustn't forget that previously, he was harmless and honest. It was Dread, and Dread alone, who put him on the road to crime. And so I feel sympathy for him, in his struggle against Dread. Don't you feel the same way?"

"No, not at all. Our duty is to hand the criminal over to the forces of the law, regardless of who or what turned him into a criminal."

There was another short silence Then Hameed asked, "Is Dread trying to blackmail some rich woman here?"

"Yes, he is. I don't know who the woman is... But I do know that he's demanding two crores from her."

As usual, Hameed was quickly getting bored with the business talk. "I'd love to dance the rumba with you," he said.

"I'm sorry, Captain," she said quietly, "but I've made my vow. I'm going to live the rest of my life as a nun."

Hameed was about to say something when four servants arrived, bearing a large wooden crate. Apparently, they were taking it into the storeroom. One of the servants missed a step, and a corner of the heavy crate hit one of the pillars that supported the ceiling, damaging the plaster.

"You fools!" Hameed bellowed. "Your carelessness in peeling away this plaster may lead to your own skins being peeled off! But what is this box? What does it contain?"

"Colonel Saheb sent it," one of servants said.

Hameed again turned to Mary and said:

"Do you see? Just a teeny bit of the plaster has come off, but when the Colonel Saheb arrives soon, the first thing he'll notice is the damage. Nothing escapes that man's eye, not even the least little bit of straw. Now tell me, is there any woman in the world who would want to marry him?"

"I think it's admirable to be so mindful of small details."

"Yes, that's all right for you to say. For you intend to live a life of celibacy."

She didn't deign to reply; instead, she picked up her Bible and began to turn its pages. Hameed made a face and began charging his pipe.

Faridi came back at six o'clock sharp. He walked directly to where Hameed and Mary were chatting and did exactly as Hameed had predicted. Noticing the spot where the pillar was damaged, he asked, "What happened here? Why is the plaster broken?"

"You should put that question to the crate," Hameed said airily. "Then the crate will most likely reply that you should put the question to the servants. But you mustn't ever ask the servants, for then they will think: how can such an important man be bothered about such an unimportant little thing?"

"Stop babbling. What's this crate you're going on about?"

"The one that you sent. Do you want me to repeat that in Latin?"

"I never sent any crate!"

"What?!" Hameed sprang up from his chair. "But the crate is there, in the storeroom."

Faridi rushed up to the storeroom, with Hameed following closely. He pointed to the box. It was stoutly made, of Indian teakwood—about two-and-a-half feet tall, four feet long, and three feet wide. Faridi opened. The crate was empty.

Hameed's voice failed him at first. Then he said haltingly: "Good God! I don't suppose... the crate itself is so heavy that it needed four men... just to lug it around?"

Faridi reflected for a brief moment. Then he said: "Have all the gates closed. Ask Naseer and three others to take out the rifles and spread themselves out in the grounds out back. As for the front, the dogs are already there."

"Am I to understand that someone has entered this house inside this crate?"

"Hurry. Don't talk," Faridi said, but then he made a gesture for Hameed to stay put. He was staring hard at the packing cases and pinewood chests that were heaped in the corner. He put his index finger to his lips, commanding Hameed to keep absolutely quiet. Then he stepped gingerly toward the corner. Suddenly, Hameed saw the boxes fall, one cluttering down over the other.

Bewildered, Hameed lunged forward. Faridi had someone by his feet. Faridi gave a powerful jerk, as one would handle a snake by its tail. But the mysterious intruder stayed stuck to the floor, just like a snake that holds fast in its burrow. Faridi gave another, more powerful jerk, and the man turned, just like a snake ready to strike.

But Faridi struck even faster than a snake, and caught the intruder by the neck, first with one hand, and then with both. Hameed cried out in surprise.

It was Finch, dangling from Faridi's hands, trying desperately to somehow reach Faridi's neck with his hands.

"Hurl the bastard to the ground!" Hameed screamed like a cheerleader. "Let his bones be shattered to powder!"

For some reason, Faridi failed to follow Hameed's advice. Or perhaps Finch didn't allow Faridi do so. Faridi simply tightened his grip on Finch's neck, as the little man struggled furiously for several minutes. Then his body became slack, his bulging eyes closed, and his neck slumped to one side.

Faridi came out to the inner verandah, holding Finch by the neck, the way a cat holds a freshly killed chameleon in its jaws. Finch had stopped breathing.

The moment Mary's eyes fell on him, she screamed in fear and shock. "That... that's Finch!" she stammered.

"Yes," Faridi smiled, "I know him well."

"Perhaps... is he... is he dead?"

"Yes, perhaps," Faridi answered, looking Finch over from head to foot. He said to Hameed, "He came for the blue bag, I should think."

"I grieve for him," Mary said in a choked voice. "He wasn't able to achieve the goal for which he had adopted his present way of life."

Faridi dropped Finch's body on the floor. "I, too, am sorry," he said.

Hameed felt strange, looking at Finch's body. His

heart did not want to accept that this was really the same Finch who had challenged them to a race a few nights ago. His now corpse looked no different from that of a crippled beggar, dead from exposure to the bitter cold on a city sidewalk.

"I will always remember his deeds," Faridi told Mary. "I've never met a bolder, more audacious criminal. But judging from his folly today, all those valiant achievements seem like those of a child pretending to be an old man by wearing a false moustache."

Hameed suddenly felt sad for Finch. He couldn't tell why. The servants stood around quietly, blinking their eyes. Something like a mournful air pervaded the house. Then, suddenly, everybody saw something happening, as fast as a flash of lightning.

Finch sprang from his prone position and hurled himself through a door. In the next instant he had cleared the corridor and launched himself onto the front verandah.

"Catch him!" Hameed cried, racing after him. Faridi began sprinting as well. But by that time Finch had made it to the other side of the portico and was streaking across the front lawn. A whole pack of ferocious hounds bounded after him, but Finch left them all behind.

Then he stumbled and missed a step. That was enough for the hounds. They caught up to him and hurled themselves upon him. Faridi and the rest watched from far, but Hameed felt that Faridi looked somewhat worried and apprehensive. He realized that when Finch had sprung up to escape, Faridi had given a spontaneous burst of laughter, as if he was pleased that Finch had deceived him.

Now, again, Hameed saw Faridi laugh with pleasure. For Finch was in face-to-face combat with the hounds. One of his hands held a sharp, shiny knife; in his other hand, he held his jacket, which he had removed with astonishing dexterity while retreating from the dogs.

By now, a number of the hounds had suffered wounds. "If he manages to escape with his life, I won't even mourn the death of those fine hounds," Faridi said, agitated, turning toward Hameed. Hameed had his gun out. Faridi struck his gun hand and warned, "What are you doing? Wouldn't you be ashamed to shoot at him while he's in this position?"

"Why don't you call off the hounds?" Mary said tearfully.

"They won't obey me now, for nearly all of them are wounded. Their blood is up."

"I'll rescue him!" Mary said, running forward blindly, in a craze.

Faridi gripped her arm and admonished her, "Don't be foolish. If you tried to tackle them now, we wouldn't recover even a single shred of your body."

"Let me go! Let go...!" she screamed and howled, as if she had lost her mind. Or perhaps she really *was* out of her mind; she was becoming wildly hysterical. "Finch! Finch!" she raved on. "My child! I'm coming... my child, my son... my son!"

Then she fell unconscious, her body falling limp on Faridi's shoulder.

Finch was still engaged in combat with the hounds, his vigour undiminished. Three of the dogs were half-paralyzed and were dragging their bodies. Finch's knife must have found a nerve in their spines. Faridi dropped the unconscious girl on the lawn, and became absorbed in the fight, like a child fascinated by an acrobat. Not only Faridi, but everyone present was watching the fight with rapt attention.

Now the remaining dogs showed clear signs of exhaustion. Sensing this, Finch suddenly feinted, confusing the animals. That one second was enough for him. He was free, sprinting across the lawns. Then he shimmied up a tree and jumped across to the next one.

"Good Lord!" Faridi said breathlessly. "He's even more nimble than a cat or a monkey."

Then they saw Finch jumping from tree to tree, just like a monkey, heading for the boundary wall. Some of the dogs pursued him to the trees into which he had jumped, where they circled around in helpless rage. A few other dogs were pulling and tearing at the jacket that Finch had left behind.

In a manner of seconds, Finch was standing on the boundary wall. He stood in clear view of everyone and raised a hand in farewell. Then he jumped to the other side.

Faridi's absorption was over. Laughing with pleasure, he said to Hameed, "Did you see that?" Then he stepped forward to his hounds, telling Hameed over his shoulder to have Mary Singleton taken inside, and to bring the doctor to attend to her.

● ● ●

The night was dark. Anwar was loitering near the servants' quarters in Irshad Manzil. It was his fourth day of watching over the Dunkitales. They arrived every day, but never according to any fixed timings. They seemed to be able to visit any time they liked, and were never refused admittance or sent away without meeting Begum Irshad in person. Shaheena, though, avoided them. Her lips would curl up in distaste the moment she saw them.

Once, during a phone conversation with Begum Irshad, Anwar had asked her about the Dunkitales.

"I can't understand what sort of men they are," she had said. "I don't know why they keep coming here every day, even after our business deal was clinched. At first, they claimed to be pressed for time, and were keen to go back to England early. That's why they were in a rush to sign all the business agreements. But now it seems as if they're planning to settle here."

"Where are they staying?"

"At the Niagara."

"That tallies—I verified that they were registered there myself. But the problem is, I've never found them there. I've checked several times. They do have two rooms there, but they're rarely seen. I don't believe they've spent a single night under that roof."

"Anwar," she said warmly, "you really are working hard. But remember, finding the man with the red mark on his wrist is just as important as finding the blackmailer. Consider that one lakh rupees as yours. Over and above that, you may also submit your expense accounts."

"There's no comparing a mere one lakh with the two crores he wants from you," Anwar sneered.

"He won't get two paisa out of me, even if I'm annihilated!"

Anwar hadn't made much progress since that phone conversation with Begum Irshad. He had been working hard enough, but he had nothing to show for it. And yet he was certain that something was about to happen tonight. He had noticed several new, odd things during the day. For one, he found a long rubber hose lying in the thick shrubbery behind the servants' quarters. Initially, he though it might have been lying there before, and there was nothing significant about it. But when he examined the hose carefully, he found that it was quite new—it showed no signs of having been exposed to the weather. He also found some strange tools cached in a corner behind the building—tools that he felt sure were house-breaking implements.

Anwar left everything where he found it. He had a fleeting idea that he should report his discoveries to Faridi. But if he did that, he might have to give back the fifty thousand retainer that was going to make his life luxurious, if only for a few days! But at the same time, he knew that acting on his own could very well make a mess of the situation.

He pondered and pondered, finally coming to the conclusion that he need not inform Faridi. In the past, he'd successfully completed many a major investigative venture on his own, without needing anybody else's help. He believed that this case could develop along one of just two lines: He would be either up one trick, or down one. If he went up, the forty thousand retainer would be his, with the promise of more to follow. If he went down one— well, it was no loss to him.

Begum Irshad didn't seem such an oppressed woman anyway. After all, why would she want to keep the identity of the man with the wrist-mark hidden from the police, when she herself was searching for him everywhere? The man must be very important to her, or why would she be willing to spend so much on him? It seemed to Anwar that she was more scared of the police than of the blackmailer. So even if she ended up in a ditch, she didn't really deserve any sympathy. She should pay for her crimes, whatever they were.

So Anwar finally decided to play his cards close to his chest. As night began to fall, he became extremely cautious. When all the servants retired to their tenements, Anwar crawled out of his tiny room. It was pitch black outside. This part of the grounds was generally devoid of lighting, but tonight, it seemed even darker than usual. He crawled out to where he had noticed the hose during the day. He groped and felt everywhere, but there was no trace of it. He paused for a few seconds to regain his bearings and then crawled ahead, searching for the hose, but it was nowhere to be found. He decided not to go farther, for there was always the danger of poisonous creatures.

Just as he turned to go, he smelled something strange: somewhat sweet, but cloying, strong enough to distract the mind and disrupt one's ability to think clearly. He held his breath and backtracked as fast as he could, and only inhaled again when he couldn't help himself. Now he knew the purpose of the hose: the servants' quarters were being filled with synthelyc gas, so as to incapacitate them. No doubt, this night would prove tumultuous.

Anwar was now far enough from the servants' quarters to try breathing deeply again. He stood behind a large bush of flowering jasmine. The air here seemed clean and devoid of the gas.

Now he ran, fast and bending low, for the back door of Irshad Manzil. But he was late, for he found the back door standing open. The mysterious party had achieved its work already. He paused to consider whether he should go in, or wait outside for further developments. Or should he find some other route to go inside? Finally, he shook his head, and decided that time was of the essence.

He entered. The door opened onto a long, deserted corridor; it was dark. It appeared to be the same corridor in which Dunkitale Junior had played the practical joke on him. He went ahead without making a sound. Then he was obliged to stop.

The door to one of the rooms at the side of the corridor was open, and light was spilling out from it into the hallway. He crept forward, slowly, hugging the wall. Reaching the open door, he halted and listened carefully for sounds of someone inside. Satisfied that the room was unoccupied, Anwar slid into it and closed the door.

The room was empty. A table with a phone caught

Anwar's attention. The phone receiver was off the cradle; it was lying on the table, as if somebody had been in a hurry. Then he noticed a woman's bedroom slipper under the table—a slipper of fine workmanship, and with an expensive instep and a velvet lining of high quality. He looked for the other slipper, but did not find it. Anwar deduced that some woman had been abducted from this room forcibly, perhaps caught off-guard while she was on the phone. It looked as if she had dropped the receiver, or else it was forcibly taken from her—and she had lost the slipper in the ensuing struggle.

Anwar left his own shoes in the room and came out fast, traversing the corridor quickly and silently. The corridor led to the large hall where the birthday celebration had taken place. The door to the hall was closed, but light was filtering through the glazed paneling. Anwar was almost at the door when his foot touched something soft. He jumped back, startled, only to find that it was the other velvet-lined slipper.

Anwar crept up to the door and peeked inside. The scene he witnessed there confirmed his suspicions. Besides Begum Irshad and Shaheena, there were three men in the hall. Two of them wore black masks that hid their faces completely; the third, who wore no mask, was a feeble-looking man, quite tall and thin. He had an unkempt beard and wore a long, yellow cloak. Begum Irshad was in a nightdress, and barefoot. Anwar figured that the slipper he had found must have been hers.

One of the masked men was saying to the yellow-cloaked one, "Roll up your right sleeve and show me your wrist."

Obediently, the yellow-cloaked one rolled up his right sleeve. Anwar was startled—even from a distance, he could see the dark red rupee-sized mark on his right wrist.

"I don't understand. What are you saying?" Begum Irshad said to the masked man. Anwar heard no trace of weakness or apprehension in her voice. Shaheena, on the other hand, seemed overcome by terror.

"This is no empty threat, Begum Irshad," the first masked man snarled. "I have the letters that you wrote to the blackmailer."

Begum Irshad said nothing. She tried to stare down the masked man. This whole while, the feeble looking yellow-cloaked one was looking lasciviously at Shaheena and licking his lips. Shaheena cast him an occasional hateful glance.

Finally, Begum Irshad broke the silence. "Just let me take a look at those letters. Let me see what they say," she said sarcastically.

"Don't try to be clever," the first masked man sneered. "I'll hand the letters over to you as soon as you get my two crores of rupees ready. It's hardly anything to you. Who knows how many years of life are left to you anyway? The future of your daughter..."

"Hey! Leave the girl out of it!" A voice came from one of the doors on the far side. The jaunty form of Dunkitale Junior appeared in the doorway. He had a gun in his hand. Dunkitale Senior was just behind him, and he hadn't forgotten his gun, either.

"Wonderful! Today, finally, the thief has been caught in our net," Roger Dunkitale said. "Remove their masks!" he ordered his son.

The younger Dunkitale advanced towards the masked men. Anwar was watching the drama unfold in wonder. *Should I jump into the fray?* he asked himself... but then he thought better of it. Roger Dunkitale was wearing an unusual sort of dress, rather outlandish, with a large leather sack hung on his belt. The two masked men put their hands in the air. Hunter Dunkitale had them both unmasked in no time.

"Aha! Sam!" the older Dunkitale said. "I thought I'd found Craig. Sam, you fool, this other fellow here isn't really the Doctor! *I* am Doctor Dread! I've been in hiding for the whole of the last year, while this petty thief here has been cheating and deceiving you. Not wanting to be demeaned and insulted by that fellow Finch, I thought it better to disappear. Sam, you idiot! Why are you gawking and gaping? Come on, let this wretched imposter have it!"

Sam stood speechless, blinking his eyes. Suddenly, someone jumped down into the room with a thud. Anwar's eyes opened wide with wonder.

It was a tiny little man, holding a knife in his hand. He held it by the blade, in the manner of a professional thrower. Catching sight of Dunkitale Senior, he bared his teeth like a monkey, and without regard to the gun in the old man's hand, he hurled himself at him.

Anwar was wonderstruck by the old man's speed. In fact, he couldn't figure out exactly how it happened—the little man jumped directly at him, but instead he landed in the sack that was hanging from the old man's belt. Roger Dunkitale still had his gun pointed at the two unmasked men.

Now Dunkitale Senior pulled the drawstrings of the bag shut, saying, "So! Now you can get some rest inside there! Of course you're welcome to test the sharpness of your knife on the bag. I promise that I won't kill you, even if you manage to cut your way out."

He put the bag aside, then bellowed at Sam: "Sam, you useless bastard, why don't you take your revenge on this imposter who's been humiliating you for the past year?"

"He's lying," said the other man, pointing to Roger Dunkitale.

"You're right, you petty thief, I'm lying! Look sharp,

Sam!" This time, Sam heeded the call and sprang at the man.

"What are you doing, you stupid son of a bitch?" he shouted at Sam.

"You're a fake!" Sam said through clenched teeth. "You're just made up to look like Doctor Dread. The great Doctor would never be afraid of a little insect like Finch."

"I'll kill you, Sam! Come to your senses, you fool!" the other man snarled.

Then, Anwar saw, they were at each other's throats. What a strange game, Anwar thought. He had his pistol loaded and ready to go, but he was content to watch, for he knew that he could come to Begum Irshad's help whenever it became necessary. He could take down every one of them from behind the door. He noticed that the feeble yellow-cloaked angel was taking nobody's side. He simply leaned against the back of his chair, looking on with wide-open eyes. Then Anwar's eyes fell on the bag, inside which the captive was hopping around. The other two men fought on, while Shaheena and Begum Irshad clung to each other, trembling with fear.

Then somehow, the mouth of the bag fell open. The tiny man came out, and with lightning speed, he was between the fighters. A horrible scream rang through the hall. The man Sam had been fighting fell to the ground, his hands pressed against a wound in his stomach.

The little man threw away his knife. He raised his hands, turned around, and said to Roger Dunkitale: "Now, sir, you can have the satisfaction of putting me under arrest... Colonel Faridi."

The man who had called himself Roger Dunkitale lowered his gun.

Sam, his eyes open wide, was staring at the "old man" in shock. Indeed, everyone present appeared stunned—

except the yellow-cloaked angel, who showed no change in expression.

"Finch, what you did was wrong," Faridi said to the little man.

"And I am ready to be punished for it," Finch said, and kept his hands in the air, although the gun was no longer pointed at him.

Anwar was as shocked as the rest of them to hear the little man speak Faridi's name. Had he not heard that name, he might have barged into the hall firing his gun recklessly. Instead, he opened the door, and walked in slowly.

Hunter Dunkitale—who, of course, was really Hameed in disguise—was putting his handcuffs on Sam.

Begum Irshad rose all of a sudden, and asked the old man in a trembling voice, "Are you really Colonel Faridi?"

"Yes, Begum Irshad, I am," he replied. "Do you remember the night we met at your gate?"

"Yes."

"You had just returned from a futile search... for this man." He pointed to the yellow-cloaked angel, who still stood in the same posture, gazing at the scene with his eyes opened wide.

"I see. So you're here with the same story!" Begum Irshad tried to smile derisively.

Then Hameed turned toward Anwar—who was still in disguise—and asked, "Who are you?"

"Your uncle, my son," Anwar said, switching back to Urdu.

"Get out," Hameed said, brandishing his gun.

"Anwar," Faridi now addressed him, "you've been a few steps behind me this whole time."

Anwar said nothing. He was bending over the body of Doctor Dread.

"So is he dead or not?" Faridi asked casually.

"He's cold," Anwar said.

"Finished by an expert hand, Colonel!" Finch shouted triumphantly, like a child whose achievement has finally been acknowledged by his elders.

"Shut up!" Faridi said angrily. Then, turning to Begum Irshad, he said, "You had better present your own wrists for the handcuffs, now."

Begum Irshad was furious. "You can't be serious."

"I have your letters, and all the other relevant papers." Faridi smiled. "Finch stole them from Dread; and then they found their way into my hands."

Begum Irshad stood breathing anxiously for a few seconds. Then she ran out of the room.

"Look after her, Hameed," Faridi said. Hameed immediately ran off in pursuit.

Shaheena also made as if to rise, but Faridi said, "You shall remain sitting right where you are."

She sat down again, as if her legs had no strength in them.

"Why were you so interested in those papers?" Faridi asked Finch.

"No reason, except that Dread was interested in them," Finch replied. "For many years now, I have been thwarting all his plans. That day when my dear child's body was found lying in the street, I pleaded with everyone to come with me to the police station. But they all hung back in terror, scared that Dread would kill them. I wept, then, at my helplessness. But now see! There lies the great and powerful Doctor Dread, put to death by these tiny little hands! Ha, ha ha ha! Oh, but what happened to that old, helpless Finch? He died, then, along with his little baby girl."

"Colonel, please," Shaheena said, "Please tell me what's going on, or I think I'll die of bewilderment."

"I am sorry... but I don't think you will like the news," Faridi replied.

Shaheena fell silent, clearly dreading the truth. Anwar was staring at the little man, awestruck.

Hameed came running back in. "She... she's set fire... to the building!" he panted. "It's spreading fast. God knows how many jerrycans of petrol she emptied to start it!"

"Where? Which part of the building is on fire?" Faridi asked.

"The whole thing!"

"Don't be ridiculous, how can it have spread so quickly?"

"There's a narrow gutter that goes all around the building, next to the foundation. She filled the whole thing with petrol and then set fire to it. It's burning out of control!"

"I see. Get out immediately, all of you. Anwar, you take care of the yellow-cloaked one and Shaheena. Hameed, you're in charge of Sam. And Finch, as for you..." He caught hold of Finch by the arm.

"No thanks, Colonel, but I think I can look after myself."

"You are a prisoner," Faridi growled impatiently. "Come with me!"

"Yes, a prisoner I may be. But I would also be the world's biggest fool if I didn't take advantage of this situation."

With that, Finch wriggled free of Faridi's grasp like a greased fish, sprang forward, and ran.

"Go, go! All of you! Be careful, Hameed," Faridi shouted, and ran after Finch.

Hameed didn't feel like letting Faridi go off on his own, but it seemed that he was now in charge of steering everyone to safety.

They'd gone only a short distance when they began to feel the heat from the fire. It seemed to Anwar that Shaheena was affected more than the rest. She was close to fainting. Anwar tried to support her, nearly falling himself in the attempt. Finally, he was obliged to hoist her over his shoulder like a fireman. He held the yellow-cloaked man by the hand, urging him to go faster. The yellow-cloaked one seemed to have regained at least some of his senses, for he was casting lecherous glances at Shaheena, and was now able to talk.

"Please, put her over my shoulder... How kissable she looks...!" He drew in his breath like a sob. "Oh! Please let me..."

"Walk quietly, you idiot," Hameed snarled. "Or I'll break your neck."

Whichever way they turned, they found flames. Now the doors and curtains were on fire; and then the house itself began to burn. They could see flames coming out of the rooms. The servants and other occupants of the house were now awake, but very nearly suffocating or in danger of burning. Many had lost their orientation and were running around blindly in circles. Hameed and Anwar steeled themselves against the flames and somehow managed to lead all the others to safety.

Hameed was now outside the compound. He found a few constables and a sub-inspector of police from the nearest police station. They were responding to a report about the fire. Hameed explained to them the situation hurriedly; entrusting the prisoners to the sub-inspector, he ran back into the grounds, where the fire was attacking the trees and plants. He shouted at the top of his lungs, "Faridi Saheb! Faridi Saheb! Colonel, where are you?"

Hameed was nearly going mad. He ran through the flames, and came as close to the house as he could bear.

"Faridi Saheb! Colonel Faridi! Answer me!" he shouted, until his throat became dry and hoarse.

The heat and the smoke had almost overpowered him when he found himself in a room from which he could see no exit. He had been sweating profusely at first, but now all his body moisture seemed to have dried up. He felt his consciousness beginning to slip away. Still he called out: "Colonel Saheb! Where are you?"

It seemed to him that someone answered him, but the voice came from far away. He tried to respond, but his throat was now totally parched, and no matter how hard he tried to shout, no sound would come. He found that though he was surrounded by bright flames, everything was becoming dark. His lungs were on fire... it was like someone had thrust a red-hot steel rod down his throat...

"Unnh... unnh... No..."

He jumped up. Something fell on the floor, and shattered with a loud tinkling sound.

Then his eyes opened wide, and stayed open in astonishment. He was in his bedroom, and Faridi was sitting on a chair next to his bed, trying to give him some medicine through a feeder bottle.

"Father!" he shouted in English, and in a wild, impulsive motion, he put his arms around Faridi's neck.

"Hameed, you fool! I'm terribly angry with you. Why the hell did you have to go back? I got out of the burning building easily, many minutes before you returned. That rotten Finch made his getaway, though."

"Finch escaped?" Hameed asked, surprised.

"Yes. I regret never having learned the art of catching monkeys. I'll have to begin studying it now."

"And that little fellow, damn and blast him, he saw through your disguise, too!"

"Yes, he did—though rather late in the proceedings. At first, he too was deceived by my ruse, and believed that

I was the real Dread. Anyway, let it go. God protect you, getting you out of that fire wasn't easy—it was touch and go. If I had been just a few moments later, you would have ended up as Tandoori Hameed!"

"But now I'm okay, aren't I?" Hameed asked, touching and groping his body in panic.

"Quite. But have a look at *my* legs."

Hameed bent down to see, and recoiled in shock and horror. Faridi's legs were swathed in heavy bandages.

"I feared you were surrounded... by the flames... somewhere," Hameed said.

After a brief silence, Hameed asked, "Did you find Begum Irshad?"

"Yes, but by the time we got to her, she was charcoal. Apparently she poured petrol all over her body and set herself on fire."

"What was the crime for which Dread was trying to blackmail her?"

"A horrendous crime, dear Captain. But she was a spunky woman, there's no doubt about that. All her life, she was blackmailed by someone or the other. The yellow-cloaked angel was a most important link in the chain of events. Can you guess who he could be? Begum Irshad was searching for him, and Dread was blackmailing her on his account."

"I suppose he was some former lover?"

"Pah! The yellow-cloaked man is a son of the late Sir Irshad. So, your eyes are opened wide in amazement? But such things do happen, dear Captain. He is the son of a millionaire several times over, but he has been living in complete obscurity.

"His true story would have remained secret if I hadn't gotten my hands on that blue bag. Listen: Irshad had two wives. One was the mother of that yellow-clad so-called angel, and the other was the woman who has just committed suicide by fire. Shaheena was not Sir Irshad's daughter. She is the daughter of the Begum by her first husband, a man of lowly status, who divorced her."

Faridi paused to light a cigar. Hameed was listening with rapt attention. Faridi went on:

"This woman, the Begum, somehow came in contact with Irshad, who married her. In the meantime, Irshad's first wife had a son, but for some unknown reason, shortly after giving birth, she went mad. One morning, it was reported to Irshad that both the mother and the child had disappeared from hospital. Somehow, both went missing at the same time, even though the baby was kept separately from the mother due to her insanity. The mother was found a couple of days later, wandering the city streets.

"There was no baby with her. It was supposed that she might have thrown the baby away in a fit of madness. Still, the search for the baby continued for a long time. The advertisements that appeared in the newspapers in connection with the search always mentioned the dark red birthmark on the baby's wrist—the same mark that Dread asked the yellow-cloaked man to show Begum Irshad by rolling up his sleeve."

"Indeed! How complex and unexpected," Hameed said in a voice of wonder and admiration when Faridi paused for breath.

"Now listen carefully. The Begum had paid someone to steal and kill the baby—but the kidnapper decided instead to keep it alive. He blackmailed the Begum all her life, demanding larger and larger sums from her.

"The blue bag contained Begum Irshad's letters to the blackmailer, repeatedly begging him to kill the boy, promising very large sums of money by way of reward—ultimately, she was offering him one crore."

"Dear God!" Hameed exclaimed.

"Then, somehow, Doctor Dread got wind of the yellow-cloaked man's identity; he dispossessed the original blackmailer, and began to blackmail the Begum in turn. Imagine the consequences, if the facts had become known: Begum Irshad in jail, and Shaheena forced to beg for her livelihood.

"Well, that's about all. The deaths of Begum Irshad and the Doctor left two questions unresolved. One, who was the original blackmailer that the Begum hired to kill the baby? And two, how did Dread come to know of the case?"

"I should think that that yellow-cloaked fellow would be able to clear up both matters," Hameed said.

"Not so easy." Faridi shook his head in the negative. "Dread had been feeding him poisonous drugs all this while. His mind is quite gone. I think Dread did it to maintain control over him."

"But how can anyone now prove that the yellow-cloaked fellow is Irshad's son? For the man who originally kidnapped him and then brought him up has also disappeared."

"Do you think Dread would have left him alive? No, it's my job now to prove that he is Irshad's son and heir to this vast fortune."

Hameed said. "To think that we went around disguised as the Dunkitales for so long, achieving nothing! Sometimes I really and truly started to feel like I was a donkey's tail. And that day when Shaheena slapped me twice—I felt like a complete ass. May her hand wither and die!"

"No one asked you to start flirting with her," Faridi said drily.

"But I did manage to scare Anwar half to death—he'll never forget the humiliation!"

"There was no other course open. We had to act as Dunkitales, to get on Dread's tail."

"And yet it was Finch who finally accounted for him."

"Actually, I wasn't even planning to touch him. My idea was to get Sam to finish him off. I think it's fitting for these criminals who delude themselves into thinking they are great kings of crime to be humiliated and defeated by their own slaves. And for fellows like Finch, I prepare my special game bags. I was quite certain that he would come to Isrhad Manzil that night in pursuit of Dread."

"How did you get to know that Dread would be there?"

"My sources informed me that Dread's mobsters were busy preparing something special at Irshad Manzil. The nature of their activities suggested that this could be the endgame."

After a moment's reflection, Hameed asked, "How is that girl, Mary?"

"Mary? Her mental state hasn't returned to normal yet. The doctors have recommended that she be taken to a psychiatric hospital. She was already in a fragile state, and watching Finch get so brutally attacked by the bloodhounds seems to have sent her over the edge."

Hameed let out a mild groan, and laid himself back on the bed.

THE END